A PUFFIN BOOK

PROPERTY OF

_____

_____

URSULA MORAY WILLIAMS was born in 1911, in Petersfield, ten minutes after her identical twin sister, Barbara. Her first book was published in 1931 and she went on to write over sixty books during her long and successful literary career, many illustrated by herself or by her sister. Her books have been translated into many different languages, including Japanese. *Adventures of the Little Wooden Horse* is her most famous book and has remained in print since it was first published in 1938. Ursula Moray Williams died in 2006, aged ninety-five.

URSULA MORAY WILLIAMS

BOGWOPPIT

Illustrated by Shirley Hughes

A PUFFIN BOOK

PUFFIN BOOKS

UK | USA | Canada | Ireland | Australia
India | New Zealand | South Africa

Puffin Books is part of the Penguin Random House group of companies whose
addresses can be found at global.penguinrandomhouse.com.

puffinbooks.com

First published by Hamish Hamilton Children's Books 1978
Reissued in this edition 2015
001

Text copyright © Ursula Moray Williams, 1978
Illustrations copyright © Shirley Hughes, 1978

The moral right of the author and illustrator has been asserted

Set in 13.5/20.5 pt Sabon LT Std
Typeset by Jouve (UK), Milton Keynes
Printed in Great Britain by Clays Ltd, St Ives plc

A CIP catalogue record for this book is available from the British Library

ISBN: 978-0-141-36115-4

www.greenpenguin.co.uk

MIX
Paper from
responsible sources
FSC® C018179

Penguin Random House is committed to a
sustainable future for our business, our readers
and our planet. This book is made from Forest
Stewardship Council® certified paper.

To Peggy Tandy and all her family

Contents

Contents

1. Samantha Finds a
New Home

THREE things were happening inside the Park on that Saturday evening in May.

The Price children were running for their lives away from the marsh pools, slopping tadpole spawn out of jam jars, pursued by the angry shouts of the gamekeeper calling up his dogs.

Samantha Millett was dragging a suitcase up the Park drive to the house, resentful because the lodge gates were shut against her, which prevented her from making a triumphal entry to her ancestral home . . . and inside the house itself Lady Clandorris was writing a letter, long overdue, to her sister Lily, who was Samantha's aunt.

'Dear Lil,' wrote Lady Clandorris.

We won't go into old arguments or rake up old quarrels or remind you what you called me when our sister Gertie died or how you tricked me out of her jewellery that Mother meant me to have being the eldest, and I won't remind you that Gertie never did a thing for me all her life while she was always hand in glove with yourself and left you all, not only what was due to you but what wasn't. But as you keep pestering me I must ask you here and now to stop writing to me and it is nothing to me if you want to go off to America with your boyfriend and leave sister Gertie's child behind you on the doorstep. You must make your own arrangements for her since I have not the slightest intention of having her to live with me at the Park.

Wishing you all the best in your life at home or abroad,

I am, your affectionate sister,
Daisy Clandorris

By the time this letter was tucked into an envelope and stamped the Price children had reached the boundary of the Park, and were scrambling over the fence, sobbing with relief and exhaustion. The keeper's dogs had been rabbiting inside the wood, or Deborah, Jeff and Timothy would probably have had their heels bitten. They had lost nearly all their frogspawn, and walked home feeling deflated, as one does after great fear. They put the remaining frog jelly into the goldfish pond and threw away the jam jar.

Then they went in to tea as if nothing had happened. The Prices, like all the other children in the village, were expressly forbidden to go tadpoling in the Park.

2. Aunt Daisy Clandorris

SAMANTHA'S Aunt Lily, having raised her sister Gertie's Samantha as a baby, had grown tired of the job. They had never got on well together. Since Samantha first learned to speak they had wrangled and argued, and when Aunt Lily wanted to marry her lodger, the lodger took her part and argued with Samantha too.

Aunt Lily thought it most unfair that her elder sister, Daisy, who lived in an enormous house in the middle of a Park, and had married a knight, should refuse to adopt Samantha when she married the lodger and wanted to emigrate to America with her new husband.

Not exactly refused, it would be correct to say, since Lady Clandorris's letter had not yet been written, but that she should not even answer her request brought lumps of rage into her sister Lily's throat at most inconvenient moments of the day. One might have thought it would have been more sensible of Lily to pay a call on her sister and state her case, but when the lodger suggested this, Lily returned that she had never been invited to her sister's house in the whole of eleven years, and she wasn't going up there at this stage of her life to beg for favours at the door.

Finally, she packed her bag. The one-time lodger, now her husband, packed his, and offered Samantha his old suitcase, which Aunt Lily packed for her with all the clothes she had.

'You go up and bang on that door and say you've come!' said Aunt Lily, having looked up trains and bought tickets to the airport, and more tickets to America. 'You can be Anne of Green Gables and Rebecca of Sunnybrook Farm and Little Lord Fauntleroy all rolled into one. Seeing you have what one might call a right to live at the Park, I don't see how she can send you away. Mind you, if she does, I suppose we shall have to take you with us. But if you aren't here by breakfast time tomorrow morning, that's all as far as Duggie and me are concerned. We're catching the nine thirty to Reading and Heathrow.'

'I don't want to go to America with you and Uncle Duggie!' retorted Samantha crossly, juggling with the zip fastener of her case, which was hanging outside like the discarded backbone of a kipper. 'Of course I shall go to live with my aunt, Lady Clandorris.' And about time too, thought Samantha to herself.

Aunt Lily sniffed. She did not feel nearly so convinced as Samantha was that Lady Clandorris would see where her duty lay. But

Samantha *had* to feel convinced. For years she had been telling the children at school that her aunt was Lady Clandorris who lived at the Park. After the first few times it made very little impression on them, since she could not even describe the house, and had quite clearly never been inside it.

But now at last she was going to live there. She would have to, since she had never heard of children being turned out to live just nowhere, and there wasn't anywhere else for her to live. She was so rash as to write: 'Samantha Millett, Park House, Filley Green,' on the covers of her exercise books, and her neighbours in the classroom were suitably surprised.

For years she had dreamed of this moment, and now it was all coming true. The Park, forbidden ground to all the children of Filley Green, was to become her home. She would belong to it. The gamekeeper would not be allowed to shout at her. The dogs would be forbidden to nip her ankles. She might even invite her friends to come to tea . . .

Samantha did not expect to like her aunt, Lady Clandorris. She had not liked her Aunt Lily. She did not like her teachers very much, and very few grown-up people that she could think of. She much preferred people of her own age. Also pets like puppies, kittens, guinea pigs and hamsters, and pretty little birds in cages. Aunt Lily would never let her keep any of these. She did not expect her aunt to like her at first. But in all the stories she had read, fierce, unwilling relations were won over in the end by the courage, cleverness and charm of the children fate had thrust upon them. Samantha liked to pretend she was much braver, more charming and cleverer than any storybook heroine she had read about.

As she trudged up the drive she heard the gamekeeper yelling in the distance and wondered what she would do if his dogs burst out of the wood to attack her. The trees hid from her the sight of the escaping Prices, who were her friends, living in the next street to her Aunt Lily, and showing quite a respectable interest in Samantha's claims on the Park. On the other hand, had she seen them she might have felt obliged to admonish them for trespassing, since from today the Park was to become almost her own property. But that put her on the same side as the keeper and his dogs, loathed by every child in Filley Green, especially on the new estate that crowded on the Park boundaries, spreading little pink brick fingers into long avenues that could be glimpsed along the Park's edge, between the oaks.

Preparing a scorching speech, in case she met the keeper, Samantha trudged along the rutted, grass-grown drive, stumbling into puddles as she pushed back the trailing legs of her pyjamas, that were escaping under the broken lid of the suitcase, and stuffed the broken zip fastener in after them.

The keeper's shouts grew fainter. Much closer to her, but also receding, came yelps from the bracken-breasting dogs, happily chasing rabbits through the undergrowth.

Samantha turned the last muddy bend of the drive, and saw the house.

It was much as she had expected to find it. Gaunt, she might have called it had she known such a word, and gloomy, and very grey. Four tall grey pillars upheld a grey stone portico, while on either side of the pillars flat windows stared down at her like the indifferent eyes of total strangers. The flat walls, tall and box-like, stretched three storeys high to a narrow parapet, behind which the roof seemed somehow to have disappeared. The faded linings of still more faded curtains lurked behind the casements as if ashamed of their shabby appearance. Lichen rambled over the tops of the pillars and clung to the parapet.

But it still looked grand.

Samantha took a new grip on her suitcase, walked up the damp, grey steps, and knocked on the front door.

Nobody came, because Lady Clandorris had just left the house by the back door to post her letter in the pillar box at the end of the back drive.

That she was living in the house Samantha was assured, because the front door was slightly open, and inside, in the entrance hall, spread out across a chair, was a tweed coat, a feathered hat, partly covered with pheasants' feathers and with much of the foundation netting exposed; also a pair of outdated ankle boots.

The hat, Samantha decided, was like the house, old, but still grand.

She knocked again, very loudly, but solemnly and severely. The angry silence of the house warned her to stop knocking and go away. Absence filled the hall, like the echo of a bell. You can knock till the cows come home, the house seemed to warn her, but no one will invite you to come in.

Samantha knew just what her Aunt Lily would say if she went home and announced that her Aunt Daisy Clandorris was not at home.

'Well you can just go back and wait until she is!' her Aunt Lily would snap at her. So to save herself a walk Samantha pushed open the door and went into the house.

The hall was really more like a lounge than an entrance lobby. There was a sulky fire in a grate which was sunk deep in a chimney piece, flanked on either side by two flights of stairs, that curved upwards very gracefully, presumably meeting each other once again on the landing above. Daft, thought Samantha, you can't use two staircases at once. You would have to use them alternately to save one of the stair carpets going into holes before the other.

There were armchairs in front of the fire, covered in worn tapestries, and permanently hollowed, as if nobody ever plumped up the cushions or sat in any other position than halfway across the middle, and sideways at that. A heavy wrought-iron fireguard protected the hearth rug from sparks, and on the floor inside the grate a plate of hot buttered toast was standing, looking so unwanted that within a few minutes Samantha was helping herself, rather in the fashion of Goldilocks visiting the three bears. She put her suitcase down on one of the chairs and munched the toast standing up.

She had never thought twice about helping herself to anything Aunt Lily or the lodger left within her reach. That was what many of their arguments had been about.

Once the toast was finished Samantha began to imagine the consequences, and the thought of arguing with a total stranger who was about to adopt her, coupled with the silence and emptiness of the house, caused a slight shiver to run down her spine.

The dead-looking portraits on the walls, to which she had paid very little attention, suddenly began to appear hostile, as if every one of them was looking at her, and disliking what they saw. Even those whose faded profiles were facing in quite a different direction seemed to know all about her, and to disapprove.

She wished she had not eaten the toast, because, in spite of the hostility and the total lack of any welcome in the cold grey empty house, Samantha knew that she wanted to stay here, and never never go back to number four Greenfield Road, nor to America with Aunt Lily and the lodger, nor, in fact, to live anywhere but at the Park for the rest of her life.

She sat licking her buttery fingers, listening rather anxiously for footsteps, but hearing nothing but the footfalls of a cat coming up the passage, beyond one of the flights of stairs.

Or was it a dog? The footfalls were just that degree noisier than a cat makes with its paws ... But dogs walked, or trotted deliberately ... not tap-tap-tap-shuffle. It was more like ... Samantha listened ... no, it couldn't be ... a bird! ... or – or ... *a frog*? Oh no! Not a frog, anything but that! Not a frog in a house, in an empty house, a huge old grey empty house where she had hardly any business to be, whatever Aunt Lily had to say about it.

Perfectly petrified with fright, because the unknown always is more frightening than anything one is prepared for, Samantha squeezed herself into the chair beside her suitcase, shielding herself with the broken lid, watching for the moment when the animal – she was convinced it was an animal – would turn the corner of the fireplace and appear.

The strange sounds came nearer and nearer, and suddenly the awful realization of what it must be struck Samantha with such icy terror that she stuffed the corner of the suitcase against her mouth to prevent herself from screaming aloud.

A rat! It must be a rat! It could be nothing else in such an old, neglected skeleton of a mansion. Of course it was a rat, exploring the comfort of the hall in the absence of Lady Clandorris! It knew there might be toast in the grate! And if the toast had been there it was most likely that the rat would have eaten it and gone quietly away. Without toast there was no manner of knowing what it might do or whom it might attack! At the thought of it running up her legs or angrily exploring inside her suitcase Samantha gathered all her goods about her and looked frantically towards the door.

But a flash of indignation at being scared away from her heritage by a mere animal, however loathsome, stopped her from bolting out of the house. Instead, she ran to the staircase on the far side of the fireplace, hugging her case in both arms.

She allowed herself one single glance behind her before she fled up the stairs. And it was exactly as she had feared. A round, dark body had come into the hall and was snuffling up and down between the chairs. She had only a brief glimpse of it before it disappeared inside the grate, and she heard the fire irons rattle. But the long furry tail that whisked around the chair leg could only belong to a rat, a big rat, a very big, furry, rather damp rat from the cellars below . . .

Samantha retreated up the stairs step by step to the upper landing, and then, by instinct, rather than by reason, up still another flight of stairs to the corridor above, which was flanked by a whole series of bedrooms, some furnished, some not, but all lined with peeling wallpaper, much of it hanging in loops from the walls.

In one of the bedrooms she found a fairly comfortable-looking bed. Samantha went inside and sat upon it, suitcase and all, her legs well drawn up, in case the toast-seeking rat might follow her, even so far away upstairs as this.

She waited and waited, but no sound came up from below. In fact the hall was too far away to carry any sounds at all. Presently she grew tired of waiting and made herself more comfortable upon the bed, where finally she curled up on top of the counterpane and went to sleep.

When she awoke it was dark, and although she could see the night sky through the window, there was no moon and very few stars.

Samantha sat up suddenly, her heart beating.

The house was still very quiet, but an undefinable instinct told her that it was no longer deserted. Yet it was hardly the moment to go downstairs and find out. She did not know her way downstairs, nor whether there was electricity in the house or merely oil lamps or candles. It seemed more like that kind of a house. And she dreaded putting her feet to the floor with the blackness all around her.

How could she go and introduce herself to a complete stranger in complete darkness?

Samantha did the most sensible thing she could think of. She fumbled in her suitcase for her pyjamas, sat on the bed to change out of her day clothes, and scrambled under a soft, old-fashioned kind of eiderdown into the musty comfort of woollen blankets, where almost immediately she went back to sleep.

3. Samantha at the Park

THE next time Samantha awoke it was broad daylight outside, and the dawn song of birds was long over. She felt as if she had slept for weeks. And the realization that she had already spent twelve or thirteen hours, uninvited, in somebody else's house sent her scurrying into her clothes, to tiptoe along the corridor, sponge bag in hand, in search of the bathroom and a meeting with her hostess.

The bathroom and lavatory were as shabby as the rest of the house. Long streaks of rust decorated the bath and washbasin as if nothing else had ever come out of the taps. Samantha dared not pull the heavy chain dangling from the cistern, for fear of the noise.

Having brushed her hair and cleaned her teeth she descended the stairs with some dignity, in the manner of a visitor arriving for breakfast, a little late, to meet her aunt. As she passed along the landing below, tiptoeing in spite of herself, towards the twin heads of the curving banisters, an extraordinary sound came to her ears.

Inside one of the doors on the landing someone was ... moaning? ... groaning? ... retching? ... singing? ... *dying*? No. Somebody was snoring.

The bedroom door was ajar. Open, almost. As Samantha came abreast of it she could see the whole of the room inside.

It was much bigger than any of the rooms upstairs. Long windows overlooked the Park and far away beyond the Park, where the small pink houses of the estate were half hidden behind a belt of trees. In the middle of the Park lay the various puddles of the marsh pools, twinkling in the morning sun.

Vast monuments of bedroom furniture lined the room like tombs of ancestors. Against the wall was pushed an enormous bed, and inside the bed someone lay asleep. Asleep and snoring.

Samantha had seen her Aunt Daisy Clandorris very occasionally in the distance, usually driving a car in the opposite direction. It had been difficult to think of her as a relation – more as a possession, too exclusive to use.

Furtively sliding through the doorway, Samantha stood nearer than she had ever stood before to her mother's and Aunt Lily's rich sister who had married Sir Ernest Clandorris, and what had happened to *him* no one ever knew. He had gone off exploring to South America, people vaguely told her, and nobody had ever heard of him again.

Anyway, all the Park and the house and the grounds were Lady Clandorris's, and she had become so grand and snobbish that she didn't want to know anybody at Filley Green, least of all her sister Lily.

When the Church Council asked her if they could have the Annual Church Bazaar in the Park she said they couldn't, and when it was suggested that she should open the grounds on a Sunday in aid of the Nursing Association she said she would think it over, but put it right out of her mind and never mentioned it again.

'Thinks herself the Grand Lady all right!' said Filley Green. Lady Clandorris did not even use the village shop, but drove herself ten miles to the nearest town, or did without.

And here she lay on her back in her bedroom, making a noise like a combine harvester, quite unaware that her only niece, her dead sister Gertie's daughter, was standing and looking at her, halfway in and halfway out of the room.

Samantha stood for some while, looking at her aunt with great curiosity, and wondering how and when to introduce herself.

Since the snoring went on and on, showing no signs of abating or turning into any kind of awareness, she turned away, deciding that what she was most in need of was a cup of tea.

She walked deliberately down the stairs into the hall, thinking about the rat, but this morning the whole house felt quite different, as if some of the joy and beauty of May had seeped in through the cracks of the windows (the door was closed and bolted now) and had spread itself in sheets across the furniture and the faded rugs on the floor.

Arriving in the hall Samantha found her way to the kitchen. There was no electric stove – there was no electricity at all – she saw that at a glance. But under the window, beside a stone sink, stood a paraffin stove with a single wick, and Samantha was not long in discovering a match and setting the wick alight. While the battered tin kettle boiled she explored the kitchen and scullery, opening every door till she knew just where the larder was, and the coalhouse and the pantry, and a dark, damp, flight of stairs that could only lead down to a damp, dark and distant cellar.

Opening cupboards, Samantha found cups and saucers, some very beautiful and foreign, some much more modern and ugly from the outdoor stall in the town market. As she put tea into the teapot from a very old tea caddy, she thought she heard a sound at the cellar door. The kettle was boiling, so she rushed to take it off the stove before looking behind her, and when she did nobody seemed to be there. But instinct made her cross the room to shut the door to the cellar and when she did so she noticed a peculiar impression on the top of the cellar steps. A damp, rather smudgy footprint ... a pair of footprints, like the front, or back, paws of a small animal.

Not a very small animal either, nor a big animal. Just an animal.

Or was it an animal? Only *two* paws – and the paws were sprawled outwards. Could they be webbed? Not that rat again, shuddered Samantha, but the footprints were not in the least like a rat's paws.

A sudden draught blew the door to. When Samantha opened it again the teapot in her hand slopped splashes of tea on to the footprints, blotting them out. She shut the door firmly and filled her cup. No sound came from upstairs or below.

Samantha drank a second cup of tea with plenty of sugar in it, and climbed the stairs with a tray, very neatly laid. She made no effort to tread quietly, but walked with a firm and confident tread into Lady Clandorris's bedroom, barely pausing to knock on the door.

'Good morning, Aunt Daisy!' said Samantha standing at the bedside, tray in hand. 'I am your sister Gertie's girl, Samantha, and my Aunt Lily sent me to live with you. Would you like a cup of tea?'

4. Bogwoppits

TO SEE Samantha and her Aunt Daisy Clandorris drinking a cup of tea together on the same bed, one would have imagined they had been the best of friends all their lives. Instead of which they were arguing hotly about whether they were going to live the rest of their days together or apart.

'I can't have you. You must go,' said Lady Clandorris, sipping her tea.

'I have nowhere to go to,' said Samantha stubbornly, sipping hers.

'Back to your house,' said Lady Clandorris.

'The house is sold.'

'Back to your Aunt Lily.'

'She's flying to America.'

'Go and catch up with her!'

Their voices grew louder and louder. 'I can't! She's on the plane by now,' said Samantha. '*And* her husband is. He won't have me either,' she explained.

'You'll have to work if you stay here!' snapped Lady Clandorris after a long and angry pause.

Samantha's eyes gleamed. She pictured herself as Sara Crewe and Cinderella all rolled into one.

'*I* have to work!' said Lady Clandorris, spoiling the effect, 'and I can't possibly work for both of us.'

'I will work!' said Samantha meekly.

'And live in the kitchen!' said Lady Clandorris.

'Oh yes!' said Samantha gladly.

'I live in the kitchen!' cried Lady Clandorris, 'and I cannot bear to have anyone at my heels all day long! You can only live in the kitchen when I am not living in the kitchen, and that's for certain!'

'I can stay in my bedroom, in between,' Samantha offered agreeably.

'What bedroom? I haven't got a bedroom for you!' shouted Lady Clandorris. 'I don't want you next to *my* bedroom! You probably snore!'

'Could I have an attic, or something?' Samantha asked cheerfully.

'You can have any room you please as long as you keep it tidy and stay away from me!' Lady Clandorris conceded. 'Can you cook?'

'Oh yes!' said Samantha, 'I can cook.'

'Then you can look after yourself!' said her Aunt Daisy with relief. 'I eat very little myself – mostly spinach and herbs and things out of tins.'

'Ugh!' said Samantha unguardedly. She added hastily: 'I'm afraid there is a rat in your kitchen.'

'There is not!' yelled Lady Clandorris. 'No rat at all! Never has been. You don't know what you are talking about! It is probably a bogwoppit.'

'A *what*?' exclaimed Samantha.

'You'll see soon enough!' her aunt returned, 'and the very first thing you can do for your keep is take it down to the marshes and put it back into the pool. I do it twenty times a day. I can't think how it got here. And after that,' her aunt added, 'you can make some plans for your future. I can't bear the sight of you, and shan't keep you here a moment longer than the weekend.'

Samantha did not reply. She collected both teacups and saucers, put them on to her tray, and carried them downstairs to the kitchen, leaving Lady Clandorris to get on with her dressing.

So far so good, Samantha thought. It was very much the kind of welcome she had imagined, and everything was working out according to all the stories she had ever read. Lady Clandorris was perhaps a little bit more excitable than the aunts of fiction, but no worse than Aunt Lily in a temper, and not half so noisy as the lodger, when he answered her back. She was used to being shouted at and ordered about. She had not the slightest intention of doing all the things Lady Clandorris told her to do. But she decided to begin by appearing to be obedient, and as for moving on after the weekend, she took that for one of the empty threats grownups held over children's heads, like Aunt Lily, when she said she would give her away to a home for wicked girls at the North Pole.

'They wouldn't have me!' Samantha invariably retorted.

She washed up the teacups, hung them on hooks, and looked about for some breakfast that she could eat before her aunt came downstairs. To her surprise the cupboards were well stocked. She ate two bowls of cornflakes and a slice of ham, and was pouring out a mug of milk when she heard a kitten mewing at the cellar door.

Samantha opened the door, and something hopped and shuffled into the room, something round and black and furry, with large, round, blue appealing eyes and a long furry tail. It had only two legs. These ended in wet rubbery feet with webbed toes, that seemed to join its furry legs like boots at some upper joint. Instead of forepaws it wore feathered wings, like a pair of short sleeves, and a fringe of fur or feathers fell over its eyes, giving it a fierce and furtive look. Its tail, of which it seemed supremely conscious since it never stopped swishing it to and fro, was thin like a rat's, but capable of fluffing out and stiffening like a bristle when the creature became startled or surprised.

When Samantha turned the handle of the door it had just opened its mouth (or was it a beak?) for a second mew, and she saw that the mouth was pink inside.

'Hull ... oo ... oo!' said Samantha, surprised.

The bogwoppit, if this is what it was, came flopping and shuffling into the room, leaving a damp trail of webbed footprints which Samantha instantly recognized, because she had seen them that morning on the top of the cellar stairs.

'So you're a bogwoppit!' Samantha said, rather attracted by the strange little object. 'I don't believe you are allowed to come into the kitchen, you know!'

The small creature began to hunt around the room in some anxiety, while a subdued whimpering shook its tiny frame. It searched round the table legs, bent down and frantically gobbled up some morsels of cereal Samantha had dropped. It then stood on tiptoe beside the sink, gazing upwards, and after rising and falling two or three times on the tips of its webbed feet, it rose like a small helicopter into the air, landed noisily in the porcelain sink, and began to rummage in the sink basket. Its head emerged with a frond of carrot sticking out of the side of its bill. This it chewed and spat out, looking beseechingly at Samantha.

'You're *hungry*!' she cried in astonishment, but from its perch on the sink the bogwoppit had already seen her breakfast plates on the table. Scattering the sink basket with a kick of its webbed feet, it flew into the air to land with a wallop beside the milk jug. Within seconds the milk jug was dry, and it was homing in on the box of cereals.

'Oh no you don't!' said Samantha, snatching the box away. She locked up the cereals in the cupboard and removed the milk jug.

The bogwoppit screamed with frustration, stamping round and round the table top, leaving angry, milky footmarks wherever it went, and flapping its short wings.

'Back to the cellar you go!' Samantha ordered, but when she tried to pick it up and stuff it through the door the bogwoppit bit her. Not a hard or vicious bite, but a firm, sharp, mind-your-own-business nip that made Samantha suck her fingers and eye it with indignation.

'You horrible, *horrible* little object!' she cried angrily, looking round for a duster to throw over the top of its head. 'You wait till I get hold of you! I'll take you straight back to the marshes where you belong!'

To her surprise the bogwoppit began to cry. It bowed its furry head almost as low as its webbed feet and sobbed aloud. When at last it raised its face large tears were running out of its eyes and its fur was sticky with them.

Samantha put out a hand to stroke and comfort it, risking a further bite, but the bogwoppit crept closer and closer till it was leaning against her knees. It licked her fingers with a warm, wet repentant tongue, and she felt the glow of its feathers against her palm.

'Poor!' she murmured kindly. 'Poor! Poor! Was it hungry then?'

The creature uttered a sobbing shriek of suffering. It raised its head in the air like a dog howling, making a small O of the end of its beak, and wailed aloud.

Samantha rushed for the cupboard. She filled a bowl with raisins, cereals, nuts and anything she could find. She placed the bowl on the floor, and while the bogwoppit, still choking with sobs, ate its fill, she scrubbed the dirty footmarks off the kitchen floor.

'It's rather sweet!' Samantha thought as she scrubbed. 'But I daresay Aunt Daisy has had enough of it. All the same, I'm not going to be ordered around just like that. I'll take it down to the marshes when I feel like it.' And she called out to the bogwoppit: 'Finished? Right then! Back to the cellar with you. Back!'

Opening the cellar door she pointed very firmly down the cellar stairs.

The bogwoppit began to whimper and growl. It would not go near the cellar door, though Samantha chased it all round the kitchen. Instead, it rushed at the door that led into the garden, and begged to be let out. Samantha refused to take any notice, so the creature was sick on the floor.

Furiously she turned the door handle and almost pushed the bogwoppit outside. The last she saw of it was its capering and swaggering gait as it bounced out into Lady Clandorris's herb garden.

'I hope it never comes back!' said Samantha.

When her aunt, Lady Clandorris, came downstairs some time later she had washed the kitchen floor as well as the table, and had a rasher of bacon sizzling in an appetizing manner on the paraffin stove, suppressing the damp and marshy odour the bogwoppit had brought in with it from the cellar.

As Lady Clandorris came into the kitchen Samantha went out. She did not even greet her aunt, but skipped up the stairs to the top floor, where she arranged her bedroom as sumptuously as possible with bits and pieces from all the other bedrooms on the landing.

There was plenty of choice. Everything was neglected, moth-eaten, or riddled with woodworm. But by sheer determination Samantha dragged and pushed an enormous empty wardrobe, lined with mirrors, into the bedroom of her choice, snatched a silk eiderdown from one bed, an Indian counterpane from another, selected various rugs, vases, cushions, stools and padded chairs, until there was hardly room to turn round, and added a row of books to the top of the inlaid chest of drawers, also a set of ivory chessmen, a brass Buddha, and some candlesticks, so that she would not have to go to bed in the dark.

By the time she had finished she realized that most of the morning had gone by and she ought to have been at school. Excuses came glibly into her head. I was moving to my new home. My Aunt Lily was leaving the country for America, by aeroplane. My new aunt, Lady Clandorris of the Park, needed my assistance. All the same she had better go after dinner. Even *for* dinner if nothing seemed to be forthcoming downstairs, and there was no sign coming from the kitchen that smelled in the least like dinner.

Although there was no sign of food a terrible racket was going on in the kitchen. Lady Clandorris and the bogwoppit were chasing each other round and round the table, she armed with a broom, and the bogwoppit with its wits and a remarkable turn of speed that kept it slithering, twisting and turning just out of Lady Clandorris's reach, while it screamed at the top of its voice in what seemed to Samantha like the very extreme of terror.

'Don't! Don't!' she cried, rushing into the kitchen and placing herself between the two contestants. 'It's cruel! Oh how can you be so unkind?'

Lady Clandorris paused for breath, panting heavily. 'I told you to take it away!' she said in quite a level tone. 'To the marshes. I *said* so. It has been at my herb garden. Eating my herbs. You had no business to allow it to go into my herb garden.'

The bogwoppit crept close to Samantha and clung to her leg, uttering terrified little whimpering cries. When she stooped to pick it up in her arms it closed its eyes tightly and hid its face in her neck.

'Take it NOW!' said Lady Clandorris severely. 'I shall get the dinner.'

'What shall I do if I meet the keeper or his dogs?' Samantha very sensibly inquired.

'Nothing,' said Lady Clandorris.

'But if he shouts at me?'

'Shout back!'

'But if his dogs chase me?'

'Oddly enough,' said Lady Clandorris, 'his fools of dogs run the other way when they even smell a bogwoppit.'

'Oh good!' said Samantha, glad after all that the bogwoppit was so smelly. She left the house by the front door with the bogwoppit clinging to her neck.

'I shall cook the dinner now!' her aunt called after her. 'You can cook yours for yourself when you come back.'

There was nothing to be seen of the keeper, who lived in a lodge beside the locked gates of the other Park entrance, far away across the grounds. It seemed strange to be walking through the woods in one's own right, and to emerge on the edge of the marshes, looking across towards the pink and red roofs of the estate. Usually it was the other way round, she looked across at the woods and Lady Clandorris's chimneys sticking out above the trees. Being sent by her aunt on a mission gave Samantha a sense of belonging to the place, even though she was making up her mind at the same time not to carry the mission out.

Instead of walking across the marshes to the pools she skirted round the edge of the fields, dodged along the gardens bordering the building estate, climbed under the fence on to the service road, and made her way to the school, where the children were roaring round the playground waiting for the lunch bell to ring.

Samantha just walked in through the gates and found her friends, the Prices.

'Samantha! Where have you been? What happened to you this morning? And *what have* you got there?' Deborah, Jeff and Timothy Price ran up to greet her, saw the bogwoppit's head sticking out under Samantha's arm. They were incredulous:

'Oh it's *sweet*! Is it a hamster? What is it?'

'It's a bogwoppit,' said Samantha, 'and it wants a home.'

The bogwoppit turned its large, luminous eyes on the three Prices and melted their hearts before it had uncurled its tail or stretched out its oddly innocent-looking webbed feet, one after the other.

'Now that I am living with my aunt, Lady Clandorris, up at the Park,' Samantha proceeded, 'I have no time to look after pets. Up at the Park I have any amount of things to do. Perhaps some day I shall have a pony.'

The Prices were not listening. They were stroking the bogwoppit's stumpy wings with delighted fingers. 'Do you mean we can have it?' they asked.

'You can have it while I am busy,' Samantha said graciously. 'Take it now, while I go and explain to Miss Mellor why I couldn't come to school this morning.'

'Why couldn't you?' asked Timothy Price.

'Because I was moving myself from my Aunt Lily's house to go and live with my aunt, Lady Clandorris,' said Samantha. 'My home is the Park now. I have very elegant surroundings. You ought to see my suite of rooms. I have a wardrobe as big as a bedroom all to myself.'

The Prices were not nearly so interested in her descriptions as they would have been if they had not been passing the bogwoppit from hand to hand and cuddling it. The creature submitted with evident enjoyment. Its eyes were half closed. It kept up a quiet gurgling, half a chuckle and half a purr.

'It's better than a gerbil or a hamster!' said Jeff.

'Where shall we put it while we're at dinner, and in school afterwards?' said Deborah, anxious.

'In the changing room. In your locker. It's accustomed to the dark,' said Samantha, washing her hands just a little reluctantly of the bogwoppit. Not that she felt she had lost it to the Prices. She could always go and visit it at their home. She could remind them at times that it really was her bogwoppit, on a long loan. And when she had settled into the Park and come to terms with Lady Clandorris there was no reason why she should not fetch it back again.

Meanwhile she hurried away to explain to her class teacher, Miss Mellor, that since she had now changed homes, and her Aunt Lily was almost certainly halfway to America, in future all correspondence and any queries must be addressed to Lady Clandorris, (care of) at the Park.

The bogwoppit slept briefly in one of the Prices' lockers. Then it turned the changing room upside down in less time than it would

47

take ten children to do it. Every hat, bonnet or bobbly cap was tossed on to the floor. Wellington boots were mingled till no pair matched. Skipping ropes were coiled and twisted like some vast diet of spaghetti, spread about the floor, and somebody's orange had been so maltreated as a football that every vestige of juice had been kicked out of the rind.

Then, wailing for food, it gnawed a hole large enough to squeeze under the door, and marched, in its tip-tilted style, to Samantha's class. It waited until somebody left the room and then slipped inside.

'It's a rabbit!'

'It's a hamster!'

'It's a rat!'

'It's a gerbil!'

'It's an owl!'

A hundred guesses met the hungry bog-woppit as it flopped along the classroom floor.

'Whose is it?'

'Who brought it in?'

The faces of the Price children (the twins' class were joining up for one of Miss Mellor's Projects) and of Samantha Millett were very red indeed.

'It's *yours*!' Samantha's neighbour accused her. She had sat next to Samantha for two years and she knew her. Samantha said nothing.

The bogwoppit shuffled to Miss Mellor's chair and sat leaning against the leg of it, snivelling.

The class said: 'O-ooh!' in deepest sympathy, also: 'It's sweet!' and 'It's crying!' and 'What is it, Miss Mellor?'

Miss Mellor was searching in her natural history book. A picture of a bogwoppit was on page 509, and she came to it quite by chance. Again the class said: 'Oo-ohh!' and 'Isn't it sweet?' and 'What is it called, Miss Mellor?'

'Bogwoppit. Believed extinct.' Miss Mellor read aloud. 'Has been rarely recorded in

England, and never since the eighteenth century. Breeds in marsh lands. Diet very restricted, consisting mainly of the leaves of aruncus wopitus, a species of weed cultivated mainly as a herb. Flight very limited, wings almost powerless, feet webbed. Prefers to travel on water courses, so is seldom found far from its habitat.'

'Then how can it have come into the classroom?' asked Miss Mellor, looking at her class with new interest.

Wondering or stony faces met hers. Most of the faces were wondering, but there were four stony ones: Deborah, Jeff and Timothy Price, and Samantha Millett.

Miss Mellor was in her way almost as wise as King Solomon. She had to be, in a class that had the three Prices and Samantha in it. She knew that everybody in the class would love to have the bogwoppit as a pet (it was crying more bitterly than ever) so she announced:

'Until we find out where it has come from we must give it a home in the School Zoo. The rabbit's cage is empty. We can put it in there.'

'It's ours!' they said hastily.

'Oh really?' said Miss Mellor, looking at them very hard.

'Actually, it is *my* bogwoppit,' said Samantha. 'It came from the marshes in the grounds of my aunt, Lady Clandorris's house, the Park, where I am living.'

'Oh did it?' said Miss Mellor. 'Then I think the marsh is much the best place for it. It is a very interesting little animal, but we have nothing here for it to eat, and I think it would be much better for us to make a study of it in its own home. Perhaps you can arrange this for us with your aunt, Samantha, and now, as it is making such an unhappy noise, perhaps you had better leave class ten minutes early and carry it home to the marsh.'

Avoiding the disappointed glances of Deborah, Jeff and Timothy, Samantha picked up the wailing bogwoppit and left the classroom. The shock that met her when she saw the state of the changing room was very unnerving. She put the bogwoppit into her satchel and set to work sorting gumboots and putting things to rights, and had barely finished when the Prices with all the others came crowding in at the close of school.

'We thought you had ratted on us!' Jeff said in triumph. 'You have still got it, haven't you? Quick! We'll take it home before Miss Mellor sees it. What shall we feed it on?'

'Aruncus wopitus. It's a herb. My aunt, Lady Clandorris grows herbs in her garden. I'll bring you some!' Samantha promised. 'But you have got to remember it's really mine and one day I'll want it back.'

Fondly she kissed the top of the bogwoppit's head. She turned a deaf ear to its cries as it stretched after her with claw, short wing and beak, and fled from the school yard, reminding herself with some satisfaction that she would soon have been twenty-four hours in her new home, and might almost be said to belong there.

5. End of a Bogwoppit

THE PRICES went home, carrying the shivering bogwoppit in turns. Their mother took it straight to her heart. The large and limpid eyes of bogwoppits were made to melt the hearts of all mothers and most children on sight.

The bogwoppit crawled into her arms, trampled up her bosom, hid its face under her chin, and cried.

'The *poor* little thing!' said Mrs Price, cuddling it. 'What a terrible day it must have had at school! You ought to have let Samantha put it back in the marsh! I believe it is very hungry. What does it eat?'

'Aruncus wopitus. But we can try cornflakes till Samantha gets some,' said Deborah.

They tried cornflakes, and porridge oats, and bread and butter, and stewed apple. Nothing agreed with the bogwoppit. It ate a few mouthfuls, then wailed and moaned and suffered as if it had more stomach ache than it could bear.

'Ring up Samantha at her Aunt Lily's,' said Mrs Price, concerned by the crying.

'She isn't there. She's gone! She's living with Lady Clandorris at the Park!' the children explained, 'and Lady Clandorris isn't on the telephone.'

'Poor child!' said Mrs Price. She felt nearly as sorry for Samantha as she did for the bogwoppit.

When the Prices' father came home he took one look at the bogwoppit and said: 'Take it back where it belongs! Put it through a hole in the hedge and it will find its way home. You see if it doesn't!'

'But it can't!' the children shouted. 'It can only travel on water!'

'Then put it in the river!' said their father, irritated by the sobbing cries.

'Be kind, dear! It doesn't belong to the river!' said Mrs Price, rocking the bogwoppit like a baby.

'Well stop it making that perishing noise!' said their father, 'I want my tea. And which of you has been throwing cereals all over the floor?'

The children snatched up the bogwoppit and left the house, thinking it might be better to follow their father's advice and give the creature a chance to find its own way home.

'I don't mind going to the marsh pool again and finding some of the right food for it!' said Jeff bravely.

'You don't know what the food looks like!' Tim objected, less boldly. He knew he could not let his twin brother go alone.

'I expect there is lots of it about,' said Deborah. Then she thought of yesterday's frantic chase and her face paled. 'No, don't go inside the Park again – don't!' she begged them. 'You remember what happened last time we did.'

They wandered off in the direction of the Park, and fortunately met Samantha with her hands full of green leaves.

'Aruncus wopitus!' she announced in triumph. 'I looked it up in Aunt Daisy's herb book, and picked it in her herb garden. There ought to be enough there to last till tomorrow.'

The Prices received the green leaves very thankfully. The bogwoppit ate and ate them. It ate while they turned the hamsters into the guinea pigs' run and strengthened the catch on the cage door. It ate until every leaf was finished, after which it seemed so sleepy that it made no objection at all to being put in the hamster's cage and bedded down with clean, fresh straw. Its eyes were tight shut, and its beak half opened to drowsy snores long before they fastened the catch. The Prices and Samantha pressed kisses on the small round body, now stretched as tight as a drum.

'I shall come and see it before school in the morning, and I'll bring some more leaves,' Samantha promised, 'and you must take great care of it till I come. It's so sweet.'

In the morning the bogwoppit was still sleeping. But during the night it had gnawed open the door of its own cage and the guinea pigs' and hamsters' cages, also the gerbils', the bantams' and the budgerigars'. All the birds and animals had got out, and some of them were never seen again.

It was enough. Reckless of what Samantha might say, the whole Price family helped to stuff the bogwoppit into a canvas bag.

Deborah and the twins took it back to the marsh pools.

This time they were lucky. No keeper appeared. No dogs barked. The bogwoppit landed with a splash in the water, gave them one indignant glance from its round blue eyes, and sank like a stone. Not even a bubble appeared.

'Is it drowned?' asked Deborah, horrified.

'I don't think so,' said Jeff hopefully. 'But we'll soon find out when Miss Mellor does her Project. Let's go and hunt for the gerbils.'

Samantha had returned to the Park to find everything almost exactly as it was on the evening of her arrival, which now seemed such a remarkably long time ago. The hall was empty. A fire burned in the grate, and a plate of buttered toast lay in front of it, waiting to be eaten. But in the kitchen a considerable noise was going on, that

Samantha associated with her aunt Lady Clandorris chasing bogwoppits.

She went to investigate, arriving at the peak of the hunt. A damp, furry object dashed between her legs as a well-aimed tea tray caught Samantha on the shins.

'Open the cellar door,' Lady Clandorris shrieked, 'and hold it open while I chase them out!'

Three or four bogwoppits were banging shut the door each time it opened, but Samantha thrust them out of the way and jammed the door wide. In quite a short while the kitchen was empty of everything except muddy footmarks and the echo of angry scuttlings in the cellar.

'They come up the drains from the pool!' Lady Clandorris said angrily. 'I shall have to get a plumber.'

'I know a plumber!' said Samantha, thinking of Mr Price, the father of Deborah, Jeff and Timothy.

'You do?' said Lady Clandorris, surprised. 'Well, fetch him in the morning, then. Dirty, nasty little beasts! Filthy little rats! Horrible, horrible, hateful little creatures!'

'I think they're rather sweet!' said Samantha defiantly.

'I suppose you want to argue with me!' said Lady Clandorris. 'Well, I don't want to argue with *you*, and I am going to have my tea!' She stalked away into the hall.

Samantha cut herself bread and jam, eating it at the kitchen table. She washed the floor with a wet mop because it did not look very nice after the bogwoppit invasion. Then she went into the hall. Lady Clandorris was still eating toast.

'Can I explore the house?' asked Samantha. Her aunt nodded.

This time Samantha explored the ground floor. In a far room at the back of the house she discovered a pianola and a box full of music rolls. Judging that she was too far away from the hall to cause any disturbance, Samantha fitted in a roll and began to play.

She had not played long when she became aware that feet were stamping and beating time at no great distance, just beyond the panelling of the room, in fact. When she stopped playing the feet stopped too. When she resumed pedalling a dozen feet seemed to patter with the tune, thumping and stamping and beating out the time.

'Bogwoppits!' thought Samantha. It gave her a funny feeling to have them so close, and yet shut off by the panelling. It sounded like an army, yet they were only small creatures after all, and their natures seemed a lot more friendly than that of her Aunt Daisy, Lady Clandorris. Samantha pounded on.

There came a tearing, wrenching noise as a loose bit of panelling fell out of the wainscot. In another moment the room was full of bogwoppits, stamping, jiggling and dancing to the music, their small wings flapping, their large feet slapping on the stone floor. Samantha giggled at their swishing tails and waving wings, half amused, half nervous at their numbers, but they seemed to be wholly friendly and delighted with her, crowding round her legs and rubbing affectionately against her ankles as she changed the rolls, and taking up the dance again in great delight when she began to play again.

Samantha played the Indian Love Lyrics, the Japanese Sandman, Alexander's Ragtime Band, and a great many other old-fashioned tunes that seemed to belong to the period of the pianola. The bogwoppits danced through them all. Then the falling darkness made it difficult to see the names on the rolls, but Samantha took what came next to hand, and the bogwoppits danced to the Londonderry Air, the Pavane for a Dead Infanta, and Grieg's Spring Song.

By this time Samantha had had enough of pounding on the pedals. She banged down the lid. Pushing the bogwoppits back through the panel took nearly ten minutes, but she managed it at last by giving them a damaged music roll to take with them. Then she jammed the music stool against the broken section so that they could not come back. After this she went upstairs to bed.

Her Aunt Daisy was nowhere to be seen, so before climbing the stairs she helped herself to cereals and ham in the kitchen, washed up her plates and completed her second day at the Park. She really did not know whether she belonged to the place as much as the bogwoppits did.

6. Trouble in the Drains

THE NEXT morning Samantha cleared out the hall grate, laid the fire and swept the hall, mainly to make the place look a little more cheerful. She picked some sprays of wild cherry to put in a vase on the side table, then she hurried to find herself some breakfast before leaving for school.

She was opening a new packet of cereals when Lady Clandorris came clattering down the stairs into the kitchen. Samantha felt she should make herself scarce, but she had surely earned the right to eat her breakfast on the table, so she ate on, saying nothing.

Her aunt sat down on the far side of the table with a shopping list and a pencil in her hands.

'Plumber?' she said briskly, 'name of?'

'Price,' said Samantha. 'If you like I can tell him on my way to school. I'm friends with his children.'

'Tell him . . .' said Lady Clandorris, 'tell him to come and put a grid in the big drain between my kitchen and the marsh. This morning.'

'He is a very busy plumber,' Samantha said. 'He is the best plumber in the district so everybody wants him at the same time. He may not be able to come at once.'

'Tell him Lady Clandorris at the Park wants him,' returned her Aunt Daisy. 'And I shall expect him before twelve. After that I shall be out.'

'I'll tell him,' said Samantha coolly. 'I expect he'll put you on his list and come when he can.' Lady Clandorris gave her a look but said nothing. To Samantha's surprise she fetched a plate for herself from the cupboard, stretched across the table for the cornflakes, and began to eat her breakfast rather crossly.

'Aunt Daisy!' said Samantha, to drown the angry crackling of Lady Clandorris's munching jaws. 'Didn't you ever keep a cat?'

'Detest 'em,' said her aunt.

'Or a dog?'

'Loathe 'em. Nasty noisy brutes!'

'Or even a budgie? Or a parrot in a cage?'

'Can't stand birds or animals,' said Lady Clandorris.

'What a pity ...' Samantha continued bravely, 'that you have no grandchildren!'

'If there is anything that I really detest it is grandchildren,' said her aunt gravely.

'I should have thought anything would be better than bogwoppits,' said Samantha.

'I'm not disputing that!' said Lady Clandorris. 'Look here! Are you trying to start a conversation? If so, why? I don't object to answering questions if they are not simply asked for the sake of asking, but I will not be drawn into a conversation. It is a perfect waste of time.'

'Aunt Daisy,' Samantha pursued after a moderate pause, 'why don't you have a television or a radio so you can hear what is going on in the world?'

Lady Clandorris stared at her incredulously.

'Going on in the world?' she repeated. 'Why should it make the slightest difference to me what is going on in the world?'

'Well . . . I mean . . . anything could happen behind one's back!' said Samantha. 'An assassination, or an abdication, or a whole country falling into the sea! Or a war, or a terrible disease, or people landing from Mars or something!'

'There you are!' said her aunt in triumph. 'Why on earth should I want to know all about all those tiresome things? Much more comfortable *not* to know them! Nothing to worry about if you don't know, is there? Why not leave them to it and have some peace and quiet while one can? Surely you agree with me?'

'I'll be late for school if I don't go now!' said Samantha, hastily rinsing her cup and plate under the tap. 'I haven't time to be drawn into a conversation!' she threw back over her shoulder as she left the kitchen. Lady Clandorris's cackle of laughter was terribly like that of a startled barnyard hen, she thought, racing down the drive towards the Prices' home.

Mr Price was just leaving the house. He said he was too busy to go up to the Park until Monday, and today was only Thursday.

'Serve her right!' said Samantha inwardly. Aloud, she said: 'Very well. I will tell my aunt you will come on Monday. Things are very unpleasant up at the Park, with the drains,' she added reproachfully.

'Tell her to swill some disinfectant down 'em!' Mr Price rejoined, getting into his van. 'It does all the good in the world to drains. Try it.'

The three Prices were very subdued and sorry about the loss of the bogwoppit, and Samantha was terribly upset. When they showed her the door that the bogwoppit had managed to open she just said they should have fastened it more securely. When they described its disappearance in the marsh pool Samantha was quite convinced that they must have drowned it. They hurried off to school not quite the best of friends.

By missing her dinner Samantha was able to explore the pool for herself, but it gave no clue to the bogwoppit's fate. The water lay brown, still and weed-ridden, with an iridescent scum on the surface, unpleasant to behold.

Samantha trudged on up the Park to find herself some dinner, and ran into Lady Clandorris just leaving the house.

'No plumber!' she shouted, passing Samantha at a trot.

'He can't come till Monday! I knew he wouldn't!' Samantha shouted back. 'He said you ought to put some disinfectant down the drains!'

Samantha was in trouble for missing school dinner, and came into her classroom to find Miss Mellor enthusiastically holding forth about the bogwoppit study project she had evolved for the current term.

'On the very first fine day we will go to the marsh pools and make observations,' she was telling them. She won't like the keeper or his dogs, thought Samantha. The Prices' eyes were solemn with the same thought. Samantha said nothing. It will be a morning off school, she was thinking. Even if we don't actually get there, or see anything if we do.

'We aren't allowed inside the Park!' somebody pointed out. It wasn't the Prices.

Miss Mellor was a newcomer to Filley Green. 'Of course we must ask permission first,' she agreed. 'Samantha, do you think you can arrange it with your aunt?'

Samantha swelled with importance. She felt herself at the same time heiress to the Park and to every bogwoppit it contained. She had only to say the word and the keeper's protests would mean nothing. The whole school would be able to flood into the forbidden acres and all because she was the niece of Lady Clandorris.

'I am sure it will be perfectly all right! I will ask my Aunt Daisy!' she said graciously, feeling not in the least sure, but hopeful.

She went home without a word to the Prices, being overtaken on the drive by her aunt, the back of her car completely full of cans of disinfectant. She passed Samantha as if her niece had never existed. When Samantha arrived in the kitchen Lady Clandorris was filling bucket after bucket with a very strong-smelling disinfectant that she was preparing to swill down the drains from the entrance in the cellar.

'You can bring the rest,' she told Samantha, leading the way with a couple of buckets. 'It's the strongest I could get, and they told me it's the best stuff you can use for drains.'

Samantha looked apprehensively at the vast regiment of tins and buckets. There was not a sign of a bogwoppit in the cellar today, and she hoped they were not lurking in the drains.

'Let's put some clean water down first,' she suggested. 'Just to make sure it gets through.'

'As you like. So long as you fetch it yourself,' said her aunt. Samantha flung a couple of buckets of clean water down the drain. That would warn them, she thought, and they would go and wait in the marsh pools till the swilling of the disinfectant was over. Lady Clandorris followed it up with bucket after bucket of disinfectant till every tin had been emptied and the cellar almost shouted with cleanliness and slaughtered germs.

'That's that!' said Lady Clandorris. 'Perhaps we shan't need the plumber after all.'

Samantha played the pianola to an absent audience. The spaces behind the panelling, the kitchen, the stairs, were all as silent as the grave. She missed the scratching of restless feet and felt uneasy. But it was best that the bogwoppits should be contained down there in the marsh pools where they belonged.

The house felt very quiet without them.

Lady Clandorris was triumphant. She did not even trouble to close the cellar door at night. Neither did Samantha. She would not admit to herself that she hoped to find footprints in the kitchen in the morning. The bogwoppits were nice little creatures, but they were . . . well . . . they were bogwoppits! Better, no doubt, to study them as a project in their own surroundings. But playing the pianola was not the same without them.

She went to bed early, and was almost asleep when she heard something snuffling, sobbing and shuffling up the stairs. The noise was so unexpected that she sat bolt upright in bed with cold shivers running down her spine, until she remembered where she had heard that noise before, and at almost the same moment her bedroom door was gently pushed and something shuffled, sobbed and snuffled towards her across the floor.

It was a bogwoppit . . . or was it? The furry head was streaked with whitish disinfectant. The wings hung limp and dripping by its sides. Each footstep slapped a wet puddle on to the floor. The whole appearance of the little creature was so dejected, so sodden with misery that Samantha could hardly believe her eyes. Its tail was a mere rat-like streak, dragging on the ground behind it and leaving marks across the carpet. Yet in all its misery and desolation Samantha recognized her own personal and especial bogwoppit, somehow arrived to find her, after a day of disasters almost too harrowing to contemplate.

She leapt out of bed and took the bogwoppit in her arms, gently rocking it to and fro against the front of her pyjamas. It smelled so strongly of disinfectant that it nearly stifled her to put her nose close to its drenched fur. It thrust its wet chin against her face, and she could feel it gasping and struggling for breath. The familiar, musty bogwoppit odour was completely submerged in strong disinfectant, the effect of which seemed to be rapidly killing it minute by minute.

Samantha clutched it frantically, wondering if she ought to give it the kiss of life, but it seemed much more important to rid it of the powerful stench that was poisoning it. Running down to the next landing in her bare feet she locked herself and the bogwoppit into the bathroom, hoping that her Aunt Daisy would not choose just that very minute to want to have a bath.

The bogwoppit wailed and shrieked and shivered when Samantha put it into the washbasin. Then it escaped underneath the old-fashioned wash tub, protesting and biting when she tried to reach it. She had to run both taps hard to drown the noise it made. Finally she hooked it out with the lavatory brush and wrapped it in a bath towel in case it should scratch. Out of the towel she spilled it into the rusty water under the racing taps. The sides of the bath were too steep for it to get out.

After its first angry yells the bogwoppit subsided, and allowed itself to be sponged and sluiced and even soaped. The smell of disinfectant receded as it became diluted in the water, and the bogwoppit seemed to realize this and be grateful. It stared up at Samantha with its large, round pleading eyes, and begged to be taken out of the water. The last of the disinfectant disappeared down the plug hole as she wrapped the bogwoppit again in the bath towel and dried it gently on her lap. When it was dry and clean-smelling it looked quite attractive. Holding it carefully in a bag made by joining the four corners of the towel together, Samantha tidied the bathroom as best she could with one hand, and returned to her bedroom.

As she climbed the stairs she caught a glimpse of her aunt, Lady Clandorris, emerging from her bedroom in the corridor below, wearing a large and jazzy bathcap. She was carrying a towel and a jar of pink bath salts. Samantha hurried into her own bedroom and closed the door.

'Nobody except a bogwoppit could possibly object to the smell of disinfectant!' she told herself, her heart racing at the thought of the narrow escape she had had of being discovered with the bogwoppit in the bath.

She was quite prepared for the creature to escape during the night, for Miss Mellor's descriptions of bogwoppits being unable to move except in water seemed to have no bearing on the habits of this particular specimen, but to her surprise it crept underneath her eiderdown and slept close up against her all the night long.

7. Mass Murder

NEXT morning found the bogwoppit lively and playful, and very, very devoted to Samantha. Its fur was clean and beautiful, its feet and wings spruce and clean. It smelled lovely.

It rubbed itself round her legs and then lay on its back, playfully kicking its legs in the air while she tickled its tummy. She did not know what to do with it.

'If you come downstairs my Aunt Daisy will kill you,' she explained to it gently. 'And she may pour another bucket of disinfectant over you!'

The bogwoppit closed its eyes and mewed plaintively, as if it were fully aware of such dismal consequences. It vanished underneath Samantha's bed.

'So you had better stay up here and keep quiet!' she went on. 'I'll fetch you some food before I go to school, and you can just wait till I come back again. Unless of course you would rather I took you straight back to the marsh pool?'

The bogwoppit emerged from underneath the bed, made a kind of nest of Samantha's pyjamas, curled up on top of them and went to sleep. Samantha was able to fetch a handful of the leaves it liked from the herb garden, before her aunt came down to breakfast.

They were eating silently, one on either side of the table, when they heard a rat-tat-tat on the front door.

'Is it the postman?' asked Samantha.

Lady Clandorris shook her head.

'He puts them in the box. And I never take them out!' she said severely. 'Don't take any notice. They'll soon go away!'

But Samantha was much too inquisitive to ignore the knocking for long. She crossed the hall at a run, pulled back the bolts, and found Mr Price on the doorstep with his bag of tools.

'It isn't Monday!' said Samantha in surprise.

'I thought I'd fit it in before work!' Mr Price said cheerfully. 'Now then, where does her Ladyship keep her drains?'

'We shan't need you, plumber!' said Lady Clandorris, emerging from the kitchen. 'The drains were cleaned out yesterday afternoon.'

'Better have a look at 'em while I'm here!' said Mr Price, his plumber's instinct leading him through the kitchen and down the steps into the cellar. Lady Clandorris stood angrily on the top of the cellar steps looking down at him as Mr Price opened and shut manholes with a great deal of noise and clanging.

'Beautiful drains you've got, Lady Clandorris!' he called up. 'Never seen such beauties! You could drive a coach and four down 'em!'

For a moment Lady Clandorris seemed gratified, and then she said crossly: 'Well if you have finished will you kindly come up and let me close the door?'

'You put disinfectant down, I'm glad to say, like I told you,' said the receding voice of Mr Price. 'I'll just have a look around while I'm here, and see what I can find, but it all looks quite shipshape to me.'

Reluctantly, Samantha tore herself away to go to school. She remained on cool terms with the Prices, and Miss Mellor did not mention the Project. It rained, and was a very uneventful day.

But when she returned to the Park for tea she found her aunt highly elated. Mr Price had penetrated the whole length of the passage he called the drain, though the true drain was under the manholes and ran along under the earth. He had said it was the best construction he had ever seen in his life. 'Like a palace down there at the end!' he had described it. And Lady Clandorris would have no more trouble with the rats, he had promised her, because the disinfectant had done the trick, just as he had told her it would. The vaults of the great drain were full of dead rats, dozens and dozens of them, all killed by disinfectant and lying there in rows. He was coming along to bury them after tea. In fact, as Samantha suspected, the disinfectant had done its job only too well, and there was not a live bogwoppit left in the place. Except of course, her own especial and preserved bogwoppit, tucked up safely in her bedroom. It was now the one and only bogwoppit in the world!

She raced upstairs to find it sleeping peacefully, full of aruncus wopitus and not at all inclined to be roused from its dreams. Samantha's heart sank as she pictured its distress at finding itself suddenly bereft of all its family and friends.

She shut it in and wandered down to the marsh pools, where Mr Price was already digging a hole to bury the sack of dead bogwoppits he had fetched from the cellar, and at the same time arguing hotly with the keeper, whose dogs were looking very dejected, and straining at the leash to leave a spot they so openly distrusted.

The keeper left, and the three Prices, who had been watching from the fence, came running across the field to join their father and Samantha. Mr Price dug on silently. Presently he shouted to Jeff to throw him the sack. When Jeff fetched it the children ventured to look inside it, and it was just as they had feared and expected. Dozens and dozens of dead bogwoppits lay piled on top of each other looking exactly like dead rats.

'Ugh! They're horrible!' said Deborah with a shudder.

'Nasty brutes, rats!' said Mr Price, burying the sack and stamping the earth down on top of it. 'Don't want the dirty brutes in a lovely drain like that one!'

When Mr Price had gone home Samantha and the Prices remained beside the bogwoppits' grave. Their resentment for each other had died down. They were drawn together in their sorrow and distress. Deborah would have liked to hold a funeral service, or to erect a cross, but it did not seem a suitable testimonial for bogwoppits. They settled on a few flowers and a painted board, on which Timothy had written: 'The last of the Bogwoppits. Rest in Peace.'

'I don't know what Miss Mellor will say!' Deborah grieved. 'She was so keen about that Project.'

'They couldn't have lived long, anyway,' said Jeff. 'There would have been nothing for them to live on. The disinfectant didn't only kill them ... it came up through the marsh pools and it has killed all their special leaves they like to eat, the aruncus wopitus ones. They would have starved to death.'

It was perfectly true. The disinfectant had seeped through the ground and lay in streaks across the marsh pools. Round the pools the aruncus wopitus leaves drooped and wilted, their leaves a pale and sickly green.

'I think it is terrible!' said Deborah. 'To think that bogwoppits are nearly extinct and we might have had a Project and got on television, and now your aunt has killed everyone of them.'

'Your father told her to!' retorted Samantha.

'But she *did* it!' said the Prices.

'I've still got one!' said Samantha.

'Got what?' said the Prices, unbelieving.

'A bogwoppit. In my bedroom!' said Samantha. 'And I simply can't think where in the world would be the safest place to keep it.'

The Prices, wide-eyed, made no offer. They had had their chance, and they had failed. There was a long and awkward silence, broken by Timothy.

'Perhaps in the Pets' Corner? At school?' he ventured, but Samantha was scornful. 'School is full of disinfectant!' she said, adding crushingly: 'Like your house!'

'Will you let us see it?' The bogwoppit had grown in importance and stature all of a sudden, and so had their respect for it.

'It's the only bogwoppit now in the whole world!' said Jeff.

'As far as we know,' agreed Samantha. 'But my Aunt Daisy won't want it in her house. She won't want you either!' she added to the Prices. 'She hates visitors, and she detests children more than anything else.'

'Does she hate *you*?' asked Deborah, not without a hint of malice.

'I'm her niece!' Samantha said loftily, suddenly remembering Lady Clandorris's threat to turn her out by the weekend. Tomorrow was Saturday.

'If I should ever have to change houses again,' she said doubtfully, 'do you think your mother would let me come and live with you?'

'And the bogwoppit?' exclaimed the Prices. 'Oh *yes*!'

But on Saturday morning Lady Clandorris did not mention turning Samantha out of the house. She went out quite early in her car, saying she would not be back until dark.

Samantha immediately invited the Prices to come and spend the morning with her.

8. Samantha Gives a Party

'DO YOU mean ...' the Prices asked incredulously, 'that we can really come up to the Park?'

'It is my home!' said Samantha grandly, 'and I am inviting you!'

'Cor!' said Jeff Price, 'you bet we'll come! But what about that mucky old keeper?'

'I do believe,' said Samantha, 'that he doesn't work on Saturdays. On my Aunt Daisy's calendar it says on all the Saturdays: "Keeper's Day Off". And on Sundays too, after Church, "Unlikely". Whatever that may mean!'

'Wait until the rest of 'em hear we are going up to the Park!' said Timothy. 'Won't they stare and wish it was them!'

The Prices went back with Samantha, and easily persuaded her to take them on a tour of inspection round the house. They were too excited to be daunted by the general state of shabbiness and disrepair. To them, as to Samantha, the mere novelty of it all made the place seem grand and impressive. From tiptoeing across the hall they came to racing each other up and down the twin flights of stairs, and when they were reunited with the bogwoppit their satisfaction was complete. They could not get over its improved appearance, the shining of its fur, the cleanness of its paws, and the almost complete absence of the bog smell that used to make its company a little less than pleasant.

But clean and shining as it might appear, this morning the bogwoppit was in a discontented mood. It showed no pleasure at all on meeting the Prices, which was rather natural, given the circumstances of their last meeting, but even in Samantha's arms it cried and muttered, or shuffled moaning at her heels while she led the Prices on an exploration of the house, complaining bitterly when it got left behind.

It did not cheer up until they reached an attic at the very top of the house, where it suddenly made a dash into the most cobwebby corner it could find, and did not reappear until its head, fur and feathers were covered in dust, bat droppings and spiders' webs, a perfectly disgusting sight. But the expression on its face was beatific.

'Look at that!' exclaimed Samantha in disgust. 'And it was so beautiful after its bath!'

'It likes dirt!' said Timothy with some sympathy.

'It liked bathing too!' said Samantha. 'It loved it!'

'Let's bath it again!' suggested Jeff.

They raced the bogwoppit downstairs and bathed it.

The bogwoppit sang and chattered with joy as they towelled it clean, and the cobwebs ran out with the bathwater in muddy streaks. Quite evidently it thought it was having the best of both worlds.

'Keep an eye on it, or it will do it again!' Deborah warned. They made a lead out of a piece of string so that the bogwoppit could not run away and dirty itself. It protested and pulled away from the leash, threatening to suffocate, so they picked it up and carried it in turns. By now it seemed to have forgiven the Prices.

'What shall we do now?' Jeff Price wanted to know as they descended the stairs into the hall. 'Fancy us being here! I can't believe it! What would the rest of 'em say? They'd never believe it either!'

'I know!' Samantha suddenly exclaimed, with her eyes shining. 'We'll have them all up here this afternoon! I'll give a party!'

'A party!' they repeated, incredulous.

'What about your Aunt Daisy?' asked Deborah.

'She won't be here! And it *is* my home!' said Samantha, adding defiantly, 'I can ask who I like!'

'What will we have to eat?' asked the boys practically. After all the main feature of a party is the food.

'There's heaps of food in the cupboard!' Samantha said grandly. 'And while the twins go to invite all our friends Debby and I can make some buns.'

The boys sped away on such a welcome errand, while Deborah and Samantha explored the resources of the kitchen cupboards and the larder. They found boxes and boxes of biscuits, also plenty of butter, sugar and flour.

While they mixed and baked in the old-fashioned coke range that also heated the bathwater, Deborah asked again whether

Lady Clandorris would mind all her groceries being used for a party for such a large number of people.

Samantha had never waited to ask her Aunt Lily for anything she wished to take to do. Sometimes a shouting match ensued but usually Aunt Lily grumbled and took no particular notice. Samantha's conscience told her it was wrong to treat her Aunt Daisy like this but now she had gone so far it was difficult to retract.

'It is my home!' she repeated stubbornly to quiet Deborah. 'My aunt, Lady Clandorris, will be glad for me to have my friends to visit me while she is out.' But she was not in the least convinced of what she was saying.

There was an enormous table in one of the rooms, and here, when they had dusted it, they decided to have tea. Meanwhile the bogwoppit slid up and down the once polished surface, or spun like a top, humming and cackling. It kept it from getting under their feet, although the damp marks of its hot wet paws necessitated the table being dusted and polished all over again.

The twins returned breathless from their errand. Everybody had accepted the invitation with joy, and meanwhile the Prices had to go home to dinner. Samantha and the bogwoppit were left to take the cakes out of the oven and to lay the table, which was only possible when the bogwoppit was tied by the leg to a chair in the kitchen.

The third time it had bitten itself free Samantha threatened it with the cellar, that still reeked of disinfectant. To her surprise it lay down meekly, sobbing and whimpering, its large eyes pleading with her to spare its life.

Samantha felt overwhelmed with guilt. She picked it a handful of aruncus wopitus leaves from the herb garden, and when it had eaten them, allowed it a twenty minute nap on her knees.

*

The party had been arranged for three o'clock. At half-past two Samantha took the bogwoppit upstairs and brushed it with a clothes brush until its fur was soft and silky, its feathers gleamed.

She looked critically at her own dresses, hanging rather sparsely inside the enormous wardrobe in her bedroom. She knew that her best dress was too short for her. She had been nagging at Aunt Lily to buy her a new one for months. It would do, of course, as it had before, but a school party, or the birthday parties of her friends, were a different matter to receiving guests as the niece (and surely the heiress) of Lady Clandorris of the Park. With the bogwoppit under her arm she went downstairs to inspect the contents of her Aunt Daisy's wardrobe.

Lady Clandorris's dresses, like her hat, had once been grand, but were now old and rather tattered. They looked unworn, unloved, and uncared for, as if nobody had taken them out of the cupboard for years. Sequins hung in little loops from embroidered flowers. Hems trailed. Necklines sagged. Sleeves were split at the seams, and fastenings were missing. All the same, Samantha fell in love with a peacock blue, low-necked, crêpe tea gown, took it off the hanger, and added a boa in faded apricot feathers. It was hardly the kind of dress to wear with her school sandals, but these were fairly new, and the dress came well down to cover her insteps.

Meanwhile the bogwoppit had jumped on to the bed, wrapped itself in Lady Clandorris's bedjacket, and gone to sleep. Samantha only just remembered to collect it when she carried her treasures upstairs.

As she picked up the warm and sleeping body, now kitten-soft, she remembered how she had always longed for a pet of her own, but Aunt Lily had never allowed it. Samantha had loved all the school pets, and had once tamed a robin in Aunt Lily's garden, but it was quite different to having something dependent on you for everything, like the bogwoppit.

'You are the One-and-Only-Bogwoppit-in-the-World!' she murmured into its wispy ear. 'And I shan't let anybody send you away or hurt you!'

The bogwoppit raised its head without opening its eyes, wiped its odd, rubbery little beak on Aunt Daisy's aged bedjacket, from which it refused to be parted, and tucked its head into Samantha's neck. She took it upstairs and put it carefully into her bed, Lady Clandorris's bedjacket and all, while she changed into the hostess tea gown.

Then she closed the door firmly upon the sleeping bogwoppit and went downstairs to greet her guests.

A large number of children were coming up the drive towards the house. They were hurrying, and looking a little anxious, led by the three Prices. When they saw Samantha standing on the steps of the house everyone relaxed a little and seemed relieved.

Samantha stood aside to welcome them into the hall. Her entire class was there from the school, and the twins' class as well. Every child was agog with something between anxiety and anticipation. When Samantha closed the door behind the last of them a sigh of relief went through their ranks. They were much more afraid of the keeper and his dogs than of any chance of meeting Lady Clandorris.

'It's all right! Everybody is out!' Samantha reassured them. 'And I am glad to have you all come to see me. Please make yourselves at home!'

The visitors, like the Prices before them, wanted a fully conducted tour from top to bottom of the house. They were enormously impressed by the number of rooms, and by Lady Clandorris's large bedroom, into which Samantha allowed them to poke their heads, one by one. She thought it best to leave the One-and-Only-Bogwoppit undisturbed in her bedroom, and warned the Prices not to mention it to their friends. When asked if her own bedroom was as grand as Lady Clandorris's she was tempted to show it off, but prudence prevailed.

'Well no,' she said untruthfully. 'It is just like any of the others.'

Finally she took them down the cellar steps and unfastened the door of the long tunnel that led to the drains. It still smelled strongly of disinfectant. Everybody was sorry to hear that the bogwoppits had died, because now there would be no Project for Miss Mellor.

Samantha succumbed to temptation and explained that one – just one – bogwoppit had escaped the massacre, and was now the One-and-Only-Bogwoppit-in-the-World. The children seemed very pleased about this, and said perhaps Miss Mellor would be able to do a Project after all.

'My aunt, Lady Clandorris, has asked the plumber to build a grid halfway down the drain, between here and the marshes,' Samantha said. 'Then if ever they do come back they can't get into the house.'

'My dad is going to build it!' Timothy Price added proudly.

The Prices had heartily agreed to keep the bogwoppit's presence a secret, in case it became over-excited with so many children at the party and escaped into the wild. No risks must be taken with the One-and-Only-Bogwoppit-in-the-World, and they enjoyed sharing a secret with Samantha.

Samantha and Deborah's buns disappeared very quickly; so did the rest of the food. It took a remarkable amount of cakes and biscuits to satisfy nearly sixty people. Samantha and Deborah made cups and cups of tea, using several tins of evaporated milk and a whole box of sugar. Even with mugs they could only muster ten drinking vessels, until Jeff discovered a whole china teaset of an elaborate and old-fashioned design in a cupboard, but even then they had to drink in turns and share teaspoons. Some of them waited quite a long time for a drink and grew thirsty, queuing up at the kitchen sink to drink at the tap of cold water. They made quite a flood round the sink between them, on the kitchen floor.

'We should have left the twins' class out of it!' grumbled Samantha, overwhelmed by the hungry and thirsty numbers. 'It's them that made all the mess, and they've eaten twice as much as our class did.'

'Well I don't see why they should be left out!' snapped Deborah in defence of her brothers, but just then somebody suggested playing hide-and-seek, and they began to pick up sides.

Afterwards they all remembered it as the best game of hide-and-seek in the best house that any of them had ever played in. When the last prisoner had been dragged shrieking into the hall, Samantha sat down at the pianola in the far room and they danced, first in the hall and through the lower rooms, including the kitchen and the cellar, and then finally up and down the stairs.

In the middle of it all Lady Clandorris suddenly came home, not early, but quite late, as she had promised in the morning. The party had simply gone on and on and on, and nobody had thought of looking at the time.

Samantha became aware, all at once, of a complete stillness falling on the house. The long chain of dancers had left the room where she was pounding on the pianola, relieved at intervals by one of the Prices, and were wending their way through the rest of the house. She knew they would be back again, and went on pounding, listening to their shouts and yells and singing, and the stamping of their feet across the hall. Suddenly the stamping ceased, and the voices broke off into a silence so profound it was almost a noise in itself.

Samantha took her feet off the pedals to listen. Nothing. Just nothing. She might as well have been alone in the house.

Something had happened! Had they all danced out of the front door and disappeared into the Park? But only a few minutes ago someone had announced that outside it was pouring with rain, and sure enough great drops were dripping through a crack above the window. Had they all gone into the cellar to explore the drain? Or had they got tired of the party and just gone home?

Samantha bounced off the pianola stool and went to look for them. And almost immediately she realized that nobody had disappeared or gone home, or gone anywhere at all, in fact. The hall was full of children. Every invited child was there, from the Prices to the youngest member of the twins' class, but they were all standing as still as if some magician had turned them suddenly into stone, and they were all staring in one direction.

At the bottom of the stairs facing them, wearing her pheasant feather hat and a large outdoor motoring coat, despite the time of year, stood Samantha's Aunt Daisy, Lady Clandorris.

Something rose and swelled inside Samantha's breast. It was not exactly courage, because terror was lurking so closely behind it. But she felt strongly that she ought to take the blame and defend her friends, so she pushed herself forward between the paralysed ranks of children, standing squarely in front of them with her hands on the hips of Lady Clandorris's peacock blue hostess tea gown. If it came to a showdown she had had plenty of practice with her Aunt Lily, and had often taken on Uncle Duggie in the same encounter.

Aunt Lily, however, had never been slow to open her mouth and speak her mind. It was disconcerting to find that Aunt Daisy was in no hurry to speak at all, but stared at her with so icy and angry a stare that Samantha could find nothing in her repertoire to match up to it.

After a very, very long silence Lady Clandorris suddenly said quite loudly:

'Is your party finished yet?'

'Yes . . .' Samantha stammered, taken by surprise. 'They were all just going home.'

'Good!' said Lady Clandorris, moving absolutely nothing except her lips. 'Then when they have left the house will you please collect all your possessions together and come with me. I have found a person to take care of you and a house where you can board until your Aunt Lily comes back from America, or until I can get in touch with her and send you after her. Mrs Bassett will take you this evening. You had better hurry up as she is expecting you to supper.'

In the stunned silence that followed this pronouncement Samantha savoured to the full the deepest humiliation of her life. In front of all her friends, all her invited guests, she was being turned out of the house she had boasted about and of which she had been so proud. It was far far worse than being suspended from school.

Yet even as she stood out there in front of them all, scarlet in the face and bitterly defiant, two things happened at exactly the same moment.

Every child in the hall suddenly looked in her direction, and moved a little closer to her as if to assure her of their sympathy and their support, while a murmur of indignation arose, so pronounced and so ominous that Lady Clandorris unconsciously stepped backwards on to the bottom stair of the right-hand flight raising herself just a little to gain an advantage over the protesting mass of children facing her. And while they continued to murmur and shuffle and voice their indignation in an even tighter bunch around Samantha, a scraping, flopping, scratching noise came from the upper landing, as the bogwoppit, resentful of being shut up and neglected during the whole of Samantha's party, came blundering down the stairs. It had gnawed a hole in the bottom of Samantha's door, and was not prepared to be agreeable to anybody. It seemed particularly resentful at the sight of Lady Clandorris.

Hearing the noise she turned and saw it descending, step by step, balancing itself upright by its ridiculous little wings, muttering and complaining, fixing her with its round eyes full of spite and indignation. It was covered with dust and fluff from under Samantha's bed where it had curled itself up with the bedjacket.

'Samantha!' ordered Lady Clandorris, almost the first time she had used her name. 'Go into the kitchen and fetch me a bucket of disinfectant!' Samantha stood perfectly motionless.

'Samantha! I said fetch a bucket of disinfectant from the kitchen!' repeated her aunt, with the bogwoppit now not six steps above her and lowering its head as if to bite.

'If I have to pack my clothes I shall not have time to fill any more buckets for you!' declared Samantha.

The children cheered.

Lady Clandorris swept off the stairs with the bogwoppit three steps behind her and strode towards the kitchen.

'Quickly!' Samantha said, turning to her friends. 'Go home . . . *now*! And take it with you!' she urged the Prices. 'Take care of it and DON'T LET IT OUT! – I'll come and fetch it as soon as I can. Remember it's the ONLY-BOGWOPPIT-IN-THE-WORLD! – And keep it away from your father's disinfectant!' she called after them as the three Prices fled out of the front door, clutching the protesting bogwoppit and followed by all their friends.

9. Samantha Moves Again

'WHERE is it?' said Lady Clandorris coming back into the hall with an over-filled bucket of disinfectant slopping on to the stone flags. 'And where have they all gone to?'

She put the bucket heavily on to the floor.

'They have all gone home. And they have taken it with them,' said Samantha, wondering if she dared pour the pail of disinfectant over her Aunt Daisy. After all she had nothing now to lose.

Instead, she found herself saying hoarsely: 'I'm sorry. I'm very sorry Aunt Daisy for doing what I did in your house.' She was nearly in tears.

'Indeed!' said Lady Clandorris coldly. 'I am not the slightest bit interested in whether you are sorry or not.' Samantha lost her temper.

'You are a perfectly horrible woman! You are horrible to children, and to helpless animals. I hope I shall never see you again!' she screamed.

'And you are a particularly horrible child!' returned Lady Clandorris. 'I knew I wouldn't like you, and I don't and I never will. Besides, look what happened when I am kind to children! I take you in and give you a good home and you fill it up with a crowd of screaming brats as unpleasant as yourself! My home! My food! My pianola! And what do I get by being kind to animals? My house overrun with bogwoppits! Vermin! Worse than rats! The only peace and quiet I can hope for is by being horrible, and I infinitely prefer it, whatever you may like to say.'

'Goodbye,' said Samantha.

'We haven't parted yet. I shall take you, *now*, to your new home,' said Lady Clandorris.

'All right,' said Samantha, 'but I've said goodbye and I'm never going to speak to you again.'

'Just as you like,' said Lady Clandorris, 'but I had better explain a few things to you before you go. My lawyer, Mr Beaumont, will pay your board direct to Mrs Bassett. And for your pocket money, clothes and travel I am opening a Post Office account for you. Mr Beaumont will give you the book and explain how much you will be able to spend each month or quarter. You will have to keep within that amount or go without.'

Samantha's drooping spirits rose a little. She had never had any regular pocket money given her in her life, and Aunt Lily had always bought and chosen her clothes, to the tune of some of their fiercest arguments. She still said nothing.

'I expect you will soon be joining your Aunt Lily in America,' said Lady Clandorris. 'Mr Beaumont will arrange it, once I get her address. And I will be obliged if in future you will keep away from the Park.'

Samantha's heart sank again. She was very very sorry indeed to leave the Park. In a sudden spurt of rage she kicked over the pail of disinfectant, and saw its contents spreading ruthlessly across the hall before turning her back on her aunt and climbing the stairs towards her bedroom on the second floor.

She was glad she had arranged the party. It was quite obvious that her Aunt Daisy had already made up her mind to get rid of her when she left the house that same morning. So she had scored a point there, Samantha thought.

She packed her suitcase slowly, to keep her aunt waiting as long as possible, and left the room, casting one sorrowful glance behind her at the gilt mirrors, the card tables, the flowers under glass domes, the china dogs, the samplers and lace fans, all the bits and pieces she had collected together to make her own room look elegant and splendid. To be turned out of it like this and dismissed in front of all her friends! To be exiled for ever from the house to which she had almost the claim of a blood-relationship! Had her aunt any *right* to disown her? Should she appeal to the police? Perhaps America with Aunt Lily and Uncle Duggie would be the best place after all.

But the thought of leaving the bogwoppit distracted her. Somehow or other she must get it removed to, and accepted by, her new home, and with this in mind Samantha deliberately scattered all her bedclothes on the floor and went downstairs to join her Aunt Daisy.

Outside the front door Lady Clandorris was waiting with the car engine running, buzzing the accelerator now and then rather impatiently. Samantha slowed her pace, and, to be still more annoying, paused to examine the contents of the letter box, which hung underneath a torn curtain inside the hall door.

Lady Clandorris had spoken quite truthfully when she said she never took the letters out of the box or looked at them. Samantha removed the uppermost, which happened to be a picture postcard from America featuring the Statue of Liberty, signed by Aunt Lily. It was addressed to Lady Clandorris, informing her that she and Duggie had found an apartment, and Duggie's friend had found Duggie a good job, and if Daisy couldn't stand Samantha it was all right, she could send her over. She enclosed an address.

Samantha deliberately stuffed the postcard back in the bottom of the crowded box and dawdled down the front steps to join her aunt.

Mrs Bassett's house, Lady Clandorris explained to the perfectly silent Samantha, was on a bus route, so she would be able to catch the bus to school every day. That is all the conversation that took place between them during the three-and-a-half miles of their reluctant journey. Lady Clandorris could not wait to be rid of Samantha, and left the car engine running at the gate.

'Aren't you going to kiss your auntie goodbye?' Mrs Bassett asked Samantha, taking the suitcase and opening the door of 'Woodside' to show a comfortable and up-to-date interior that could not have been more of a contrast to the Park. But, before Samantha could openly refuse, Lady Clandorris hurried off down the garden path to argue with a policeman, who had arrived to admonish her for leaving her car engine running unattended while the car was stationary in the main road. While she was trying to justify her licence and insurance being out of date, and the car being on the road without a certificate of roadworthiness, Mrs Bassett quietly and tactfully drew Samantha inside and shut the door.

It was the beginning of a new life for Samantha, and a very agreeable life, that lasted exactly one week.

At the end of that week Mrs Bassett's mother had a stroke and could no longer be left to live alone. The only other place for her to live was with Mrs Bassett, and since the only spare bedroom that Mrs Bassett had was being slept in by Samantha, Mrs Bassett's mother had to have it, and Samantha had to go.

Everybody was very sorry to turn Samantha out, even Mrs Bassett's mother, but there was no help for it, and Lady Clandorris's lawyer, Mr Beaumont, was summoned to deal with the situation.

Meanwhile quite a number of other events had taken place. The bogwoppit had been fetched from the Prices, and was living in a large empty drainpipe with bars jammed tightly against it at either end in Mrs Bassett's yard.

'Of course you can keep a pet, dear!' Mrs Bassett had warmly agreed when Samantha had explained the situation to her. 'It is nice for children to have pets. My boys always had them.'

And she suggested the drainpipe herself. She was ready to admire the bogwoppit, but found it very curious. She had never seen anything like it before.

'Children have such odd pets nowadays!' she said to her next-door neighbour. 'With Trevor and Les it was hamsters and mice, but now it's all gerbils and mynah birds and things like this funny old rat of Sammy's. Still, it's nice for a child to have a pet.' And she put up with the bogwoppit's moaning and grumbling while Samantha was at school.

This time the Prices had faithfully carried out their responsibilities and kept the bogwoppit safe the whole night long after the party. In fact, they had sat up in turns to make sure it did not escape. And when Mrs Price knew for certain that Samantha meant to come and fetch it after school she allowed them to lock it up in the wash house where it could not possibly gnaw through the tin plating at the bottom of the door, though it chewed, bit and worried at a great many other things, including Mr Price's trousers, which were hanging from the ceiling. The bogwoppit just rose in the air like a helicopter and fetched them down.

But even Mr Price was sorry for Samantha and her troubles, and he was very tolerant about the trousers. At the end of the week when Mrs Bassett could no longer give her a room and Lady Clandorris still refused to have Samantha back at the Park, Mr and Mrs Price had a long talk together and agreed to offer Samantha a home.

Lady Clandorris's lawyer, Mr Beaumont, who was at his wits' end to know what to do with her, was more than happy to fall in with the arrangement. Lady Clandorris, when referred to, said Mr Price was an excellent plumber, and anyway, when her Aunt Lily sent her address, Samantha would soon be joining her in America. Deborah, Jeff and Timothy Price were delighted, and Mrs Bassett, who had become very fond of Samantha, was much relieved.

But Samantha said she would not go anywhere without the bogwoppit.

She had the good sense to put the whole position in front of Mr and Mrs Price, explaining how the little creatures in the park pools had suffered a miserable death through Mr Price's inadvertent recommendation to use disinfectant in the drains. She explained that they were not rats at all, but a very rare and almost extinct form of animal life called a bogwoppit, which was about to become a Project for the school to study, and would almost certainly attain nationwide importance, and appear on television. She explained that it was quite impossible to put the bogwoppit back in the marsh pools while the remains of disinfectant still lurked there, and putting it into a Pets' Home or boarding kennels was quite out of the question, because they would not have the right kind of food for it.

In fact the bogwoppit's food had become a crucial problem, because Samantha no longer had access to the aruncus wopitus leaves that grew in Lady Clandorris's herb garden. She already had plans for making a raid on the garden, aided by the Prices, for she was actually a little nervous of going alone. Meanwhile the bogwoppit lived on a diet of cornflakes and milk, which suited its digestion very badly indeed.

When Mr Price realized that it was in fact the Only-Bogwoppit-in-the-World he reluctantly agreed to Samantha keeping it until the marsh pools were free enough of disinfectant for it to go back and live there again.

'But it can't go back until you have put a grid between the pool and the house, so it isn't able to get back into the kitchen,' Samantha pursued, 'because if my Aunt Daisy catches sight of it she will throw more disinfectant down the drain and kill it, and that will be the end of every bogwoppit that ever was. It would be criminal!'

Samantha's arguments were forceful, and Mr Price began to think that perhaps she was right. He stipulated that the bogwoppit should be contained in a drain pipe, as at Mrs Bassett's, and Mrs Bassett was only too glad for Samantha to take the drain pipe away with her. Mr Price fetched it in his van when he collected Samantha and her luggage and the bogwoppit. Then he went straight up to the Park and fixed an iron-barred grid with a gate, in the big drain half way between the marsh and the house. The gate was locked with a key. Lady Clandorris insisted on having a key of her own, while Mr Price kept a second.

Samantha begged him to go into her aunt's herb garden while he was up at the house, and bring back some leaves of aruncus wopitus for the bogwoppit. Being a kind-hearted man, Mr Price made an excuse about finding the route of the watercourse, and opened the door into the little courtyard that led out of the hall. He picked what he guessed to be the right leaves and put them into his toolbag.

But when Samantha received them for the hungry bogwoppit she found that Mr Price had picked some quite different leaves that made the bogwoppit sick, and for two days it would not eat anything at all.

Mrs Price nursed it like a baby, bringing it back to health with alternate spoons of egg custard and spinach, but it grew weak and listless. Samantha began to realize that something would have to be done before it died.

10. A Dangerous Mission

SAMANTHA took Jeff Price into her confidence. He was the smaller and braver of the twins, and the less likely to betray a secret.

'I'm going up to the Park tonight to get some aruncus leaves,' she told him. 'After dark. Long after we all go to bed. Will you help me?'

Jeff needed no persuading. 'How'll we get in?' he asked at once.

'I know a window that doesn't shut,' said Samantha, 'and the key is always left in the garden door that leads out of the hall.'

'Great!' said Jeff. 'How'll we wake up?'

'I shan't go to sleep,' said Samantha. 'You can, because it doesn't matter ... I'll wake you. Have you got a torch?'

He had. 'And it's full moon!' Jeff added.

'Bring one of your father's toolbags! The biggest you can find. We'll bring back some roots and plant them in your mother's garden. And we'll pick enough leaves to put in the freezer!' said Samantha.

'Can't Tim come too?' Jeff asked.

'No. Two is plenty. Besides, Deb wouldn't want to be the only one left out. Just you and me,' said Samantha.

Jeff was persuaded, and felt rather proud to be chosen. All the same he slept with his usual soundness, and had almost forgotten the whole mission when Samantha crept into the twins' bedroom soon after midnight to shake him awake.

'Come on,' she urged him in a whisper. 'Don't you remember? We're going up to the Park to get leaves for the bogwoppit!'

He struggled awake, staring at her, and to her dismay Samantha realized that she had awakened not Jeff, but Timothy.

'Ssh! Go to sleep! It's Jeff I want!' she said, pushing him back in the pillows. 'Jeff! Wake up! It's time to go! Don't you say a word!' she threatened Tim, who bounced up in his bed again and appeared much more ready than his brother was to get up and go out with Samantha.

Jeff did get out of bed at last, yawning widely. He put his clothes on over his pyjamas. Tim began to get up too.

'No! Not you!' Samantha insisted. 'Only the two of us. We might get caught or seen. Three of us would be dangerous. Come on, Jeffy, let's go!'

They slipped out of the door, carrying Mr Price's largest toolbag that had been hidden underneath Jeff's side of the mattress.

Timothy lay back listening to their feet quietly tiptoeing down the stairs. He felt very uneasy, and wondered whether he ought to go and tell his father. In the end the silence overcame him and he went back to sleep. He only slept for just over an hour. Then shortly after two o'clock he woke again.

Samantha and Jeff ran up the silent Park drive in the moonlight, their footsteps on the night grass making quite a different sound from daylight noises. The moon was so bright it was like being on a pantomime stage, only the footlights came from above, not below.

The Park seemed strangely different, partly because of the moonlight and partly because, instead of belonging to it as she had done so recently, Samantha now felt herself to be an outlaw and a stranger ... even at this moment . . . a thief! Not a breath of summer night air stirred the branches. A pheasant moved in a tree. A twig fell, and a far-off clock chimed the quarter hour, but by far the loudest sounds were their guilty footfalls that they tried to muffle by running on the dry and rustling grass.

Jeff accidentally knocked the toolbag against Samantha's legs and she cried out, startled. But there was no one to hear her, and they came to the Park, standing gaunt and grey in the moonlight, not so much forbidding as disapproving of their mission and all that it entailed.

The gravel on the drive in front of the house was so ancient and weed-ridden that their footsteps made little impression. They stole across the gravel on tiptoe to the ribbon of shaggy grass underneath the downstairs window.

'This way!' said Samantha. They tiptoed past the stone portico, round the corner of the house, where, sure enough, a few feet above their heads a sash window stood open at the top, almost wide enough for a child's body to squeeze inside.

Samantha stood on Jeff's back to reach the sill. Then she grasped the open edge of the window and pulled it downwards. With a horrible jerk and scream it opened.

Samantha leapt off the sill and together they ran for the nearest bush, a laurel whose branches trailed across the corner of the house and provided some shelter. Side by side they crouched shivering, while the toolbag like a long black slug stood out large and clear on the gravel facing the open window, through which at any minute they expected Lady Clandorris to poke her head.

They waited until the far clock chimed another quarter, but all was silent within.

'She must be very sound asleep! I expect she is snoring!' said Samantha. 'Her bedroom is up there somewhere. Come on! Let's get inside!'

But Jeff's nerve was shaken, and it was another five minutes before he dared to help Samantha on to the sill again. When she was safely through the gap in the window and had dropped inside the room he jumped for the sill, pulled himself up by his hands, and clambered in after her. His teeth were still chattering with fear.

They were in the old dining room which Lady Clandorris never used, preferring to eat her meals in the kitchen. But Samantha had given her party here, and had sometimes carried in her own meals on a tray and dined in state at the long table. She could still see some of the party crumbs lying on the surface in the moonlight.

New courage inspired her, now that she was back in familiar surroundings ... surroundings to which she had a personal right, she told herself defiantly, and with Jeff a small, timid shadow at her heels, carrying the toolbag, she quietly opened the door into the moonlit hall.

She half expected to find her Aunt Daisy waiting for her there, standing in silent accusation at the foot of the stairs as she had stood on the evening of the party, but tonight there was nobody in the hall or on either of the staircases.

They ran across the stone flags to the door leading into the herb garden, and sure enough, the key was in the door. Samantha turned it. There came another creak, but not so loud this time, and the door opened.

The aromatic scent of green-growing herbs met their noses as they closed the door behind them and crept out into the garden. The shadow of the house covered the overgrown beds, edged with box. Round the outside of the garden high walls supported strands of old-fashioned climbing roses, that clawed at Samantha's hair with spiteful thorns.

'Got the torch?' she whispered to Jeff. He found it in the bottom of the bag. The battery was running out, and the pale, restricted beam searched faintly among the herbage for the plant they had come to find.

It was not surprising that Mr Price had made a mistake in his choice of leaves, for the different plants grew in such variety and such profusion and were so tangled up with one another, that it needed broad daylight to see where one began and the other ended.

'I think it's over on this side,' Samantha said, wading among the plants, each of which gave out a different scent as it brushed against her legs. 'Ah-h-hh!' she breathed suddenly, in relief, 'I thought so! They're here!'

Jeff shone the torch on a clump of aruncus wopitus crouching under the wall, and Samantha picked and filled the toolbag.

'We must dig up some plants!' she said. 'Have you got a knife, Jeff?'

He had not, and the roots of the plants were long, strong and stubborn. Tugging and jerking they only succeeded in breaking off the plants above the roots.

'Wait,' Samantha said, breathless, 'I'll fetch the breadknife from the kitchen!' She disappeared, leaving Jeff sitting like a small frightened rabbit among the aruncus wopitus leaves.

But she was not long away. Almost at once she was back at his side, and even in the shadow of the house he could tell that she was trembling all over with apprehension.

'I heard her door open!' she hissed at him. 'Get down in the leaves, and lie quite flat! Don't make a sound! I think she heard us!'

'Shut the door!' urged Jeff, but it was too late now. Across the small courtyard garden they could distinctly hear the creak and tread of feet descending the stairs.

Samantha and Jeff flung themselves flat among the herbs, their faces pressed to the sweet-smelling leaves of thyme and marjoram, which for ever afterwards they would associate with the terror of being hunted and probably discovered, by Lady Clandorris.

Lying as still as stones they heard footsteps crossing the hall and approaching as far as the very threshold of the garden. Jeff was lying most uncomfortably across the torch, but he could not for the life of him remember whether he had switched it off or not. And if he had not, surely a faint and treacherous beam like the glow on the tail of a glow-worm, would penetrate the leaves and betray him? At the same time Samantha was asking herself where they had left the toolbag, and could it be seen from the door? Also what Aunt Daisy would be likely to say if she caught them, and whether she would send for the police.

The footsteps stopped, and the silence that followed lasted almost longer than they could bear.

Then, suddenly, they heard the door closed, and the key turned in the lock. Muffled now, the footsteps died away across the hall.

After a few minutes Samantha looked up.

'That's done it!' she said. 'We're locked in!'

There was no other entrance to the herb garden, which was just a little courtyard built out beyond the house. The walls around it were too high to scale, and the roses too frail for climbing.

'If we wait here till daylight she'll see us!' said Jeff, ready for tears.

'P'raps not,' said Samantha, 'not if we lie quite flat till she goes out.'

'How long?' said Jeff hopefully.

That was the question. As far as Samantha remembered, Lady Clandorris sometimes opened the door into the herb garden, and sometimes she didn't. It all depended upon whether she wanted some herbs for her dinner or not.

'We could shout!' said Jeff lamely. Neither of them liked the idea of deliberately betraying themselves at one o'clock in the morning in a place where they had been expressly forbidden to go.

'If she thought there was anybody here she would have come and looked,' said Samantha, thinking aloud. 'Supposing she just thought she had left the door open and the wind was blowing it – supposing she *doesn't* think there is anyone about!'

'Then we could be here for days!' whispered Jeff in what was almost a wail.

They waited, Samantha baffled, Jeff hoping that she would suddenly announce some wonderful solution to their problem. The minutes passed by.

'I have got just one idea!' Samantha said presently. 'We could break the panel in the door and run for it while she is coming down the stairs! We could get away long before she caught us.'

'She would be able to see who we were, from the stairs,' Jeff pointed out. 'And if you break a window the police get you and your dad has to pay. My dad said we were never to get into trouble with the police.'

'Well, would you rather stop here all night, and perhaps all tomorrow too, then?' Samantha said crossly.

Jeff shook his head, too miserable to answer.

Samantha began to make plans for breaking down the panel, which was made of painted wood and looked solid. Both she and Jeff were wearing canvas shoes, and unfortunately the toolbag had no tools in it. She took the rubber-handled torch and began to search for large stones, but it seemed very unlikely that they would be able to smash in the panel and escape before Lady Clandorris heard them and came rushing downstairs.

And then, when the whole situation seemed hopeless and Jeff was really in tears at last, and they were making up their minds whether it was better to shout for help together or to curl up and sleep the rest of the night among the herbs, an extraordinary thing happened.

The moonlight had shifted, and now an angle of light came fingering into the herb garden, and touched the door. Noticing this they watched it, and saw to their utter surprise and disbelief that very gently, very silently, the door was opening.

While they watched with pounding heartbeats it opened from the width of a crack to a space wide enough for a face to peep through, and the face, pale in the moonlight, strangely small and scared and furtive, was the face of Jeff's twin brother, Timothy.

Tim had slept just a little longer than an hour when he awoke with a jerk to look and see whether Jeff had come home. He felt as if he had slept for hours, and on finding the bed still empty he was so dismayed that he came at once to the conclusion that something terrible must have happened.

It seemed such a very long time ago that he had found Samantha standing beside his bed, shaking him by the arm and saying – what had she been saying? That he was to go with her to the Park to get aruncus wopitus leaves for the bogwoppit – and then it turned out that it was not Timothy she wanted, it was Jeff. Jeff, he knew, was more spunky and would do anything to please Samantha. So Jeff had gone with her and surely they should have been back by now?

What could have happened? Perhaps the keeper had caught them! Perhaps the dogs had savaged them! Perhaps Lady Clandorris had caught them and shut them up and sent for the police? Something must have happened. Tim lay wondering if he ought to tell his father, but the consequences might be serious.

Oddly enough he was more afraid of the possible consequences than of investigating for himself, and it was his twin brother that he was thinking of, not Samantha. For the second time that night he got out of bed, then dressed himself, and left the house as quietly as possible. Hearing him, the bogwoppit moaned and scratched inside the drain-pipe, but it was always doing that and nobody took any notice.

Tim jogged up the Park drive in the footsteps of his brother and Samantha. The sight of the open window was almost a relief after the lonely emptiness of the moonlit night. At least it gave him a clue. They had been to the Park. They had been *in* the Park, and it looked as if they might still be in there now!

It took real courage for Tim to haul himself on to the windowsill and then through the window into Lady Clandorris's dining room. For no one but his twin brother would he ever have undertaken anything so brave and daring. There was a mite of assurance in the fact that only a couple of weeks ago he had explored this same house from top to bottom, and had walked round the huge old table just as he was doing now, but with far more confidence.

He tiptoed into the hall and looked across it. Everything was perfectly still. He had half expected to find some sign of Jeff and Samantha the moment he entered the house, but to his disappointment there was nothing at all.

Tim remembered the stairs, and the way into the kitchen, and the passage on the west side of the hall, leading to the pianola room. He walked across and looked inside. But the pianola stood deserted, music rolls lying about the floor just as they had left it after the party, and anyway, it was silly to think that anybody would be playing it in the middle of the night. Moonlight still flooded the lower rooms, though the moon was travelling on its way, and already half of the house was in shadow.

They were going to fetch food for the bogwoppit, Samantha had said, and the bogwoppit ate leaves – aruncus wopitus leaves, and the leaves grew in Lady Clandorris's herb garden. Yes! The herb garden! Samantha had showed them a herb garden on the day of the party, but where *was* the herb garden? Samantha had opened a door into a courtyard, and the leaves were in there in abundance, but which door had she opened? She had shown them so many places.

Timothy stood alone in the hall, feeling terribly unprotected, as if every door he could see was about to spring open and something awful jump out of it and envelop him. He dared not try the handles. He crept round the walls counting the doors and timidly passing his hands across the panels. If the garden door had fitted better, and if the moon had not been shining across the top of the little courtyard he might never have dared to open any doors at all, but suddenly a chink of very pale light at the top of the panel caught his eye, and he was filled with hope. His fingers met the spiny resistance of a key, but now he had the confidence to turn it, and very slowly, very furtively, he pulled the door open.

Long before he saw them lurking among the leaves Jeff and Samantha had bounded out of their hiding places, so suddenly that he nearly cried aloud in terror. Samantha brushed past him and led the way helter-skelter across the hall, into the dining room and through the window, paying no heed this time to any noise they might make so anxious were they to escape from the Park.

Jeff had the presence of mind to shut the garden door behind them. He passed up the bag to Samantha, who snatched it and dropped it outside, following with a jump and a sprawl that skinned both her knees on the gravel outside.

It seemed an age before both the twins followed. First Tim climbed out gingerly on to the windowsill, and jumped to the ground. Then Jeff appeared, threw his leg over the sash, and came slithering down. Like Samantha, he landed badly, and stood for a moment rubbing his knees and groaning underneath his breath.

As the three of them huddled underneath the dining-room window, clutching the toolbag and rubbing their grazes, poised for flight, the entire contents of a large bucket of disinfectant came hurtling from the window above on to the dark and shady patch where they were standing, drenching everyone of them from head to foot. By some unaccountable good fortune the toolbag, being strapped up, escaped most of the deluge, and Samantha washed the leaves very carefully in clean water in the morning before giving them to the bogwoppit.

As they tore down the drive towards the Prices' home their gasping breath was interrupted by bursts of hysterical laughter.

'And all the time . . .' Samantha panted, 'she thought . . . she thought . . . she thought we were *bogwoppits*!'

11. The Bogwoppit Goes
Back to the Marsh

THE BOGWOPPIT received the aruncus
wopitus leaves greedily if not graciously.
Samantha rationed them as best she could,
for she was well aware that the toolbag
held no more than a few days' supply, and
nothing would ever persuade her to undertake
another midnight raid upon the Park, nor
Jeff either. Tim had bad dreams for three
nights afterwards, and shrieked in his
sleep. Deborah would hardly speak to any of

them, because they had left her out of the adventure.

Samantha was doing her best to behave so beautifully that neither her Aunt Lily nor her Aunt Daisy would have known her. She was genuinely attached to the Price family, and took her manners from theirs, added to which she knew that the bogwoppit was behaving quite badly enough for both of them. In the drain pipe it moaned and wailed, if Samantha was within earshot, while if she let it out, unless she held it in her arms, holding it very tight and lovingly, it got into every kind of mischief, from swinging on Mrs Price's washing to pulling the weights off the cuckoo clock. It even attacked the cuckoo when he came out to protest at such treatment. The bogwoppit then refused to be caught, and had to be bribed back into its hated cage with handfuls of aruncus wopitus and some mud, so that the supplies dwindled very quickly indeed.

At school, Miss Mellor was busy with quite a different Project featuring glow-worms, but she had not forgotten about the bogwoppits, and asked Samantha if she had seen any signs of them lately.

Samantha hesitated. She felt the time had not yet come to make a Project of the One-and-Only-Bogwoppit-in-the-World. Not, that is, until it could be returned to its natural surroundings. It was becoming such a problem that, fond of it as she was, she could not help hoping that the day was not far off.

'I don't think there have been any bogwoppits in the marsh lately,' she said truthfully. 'I haven't seen them there myself.'

'Well perhaps after half-term we can make a start!' said Miss Mellor. 'You can ask your auntie's permission when she comes back from her visit.'

Everyone seemed to think that Lady Clandorris had gone away for a short time, and that was why Samantha was living with the Prices instead of up at the Park. Even the children who had come to the party thought it was only a temporary arrangement. They would not have believed her aunt could be so cruel as to banish Samantha for ever from her home.

Samantha realized that something would have to be done about the bogwoppit. Kind Mrs Price was becoming quite short-tempered, and when dirty footprints appeared all over Mr Price's newly ironed pyjamas he became short-tempered, too. Also, the aruncus wopitus had run out.

'We'll *have* to take it back to the marsh!' Deborah said. 'Honestly, I think our dad will wring its neck if we don't do it soon.'

'The aruncus stuff must be growing in the marsh pools again by now,' said Samantha. 'What we had better do is this: Tim and Deb can go round the *outside* of the Park as far as the keeper's cottage. If he is there and the dogs are shut up they can wave a hanky from the top of the back gates. We can see it if we climb on the fence this side of the Park. And if he's out and about they needn't wave at all. Then we'll know not to do it just then. It's quite safe. There's no law against waving handkerchiefs on a Saturday afternoon, not from anybody's back gate. He can't get them for that!'

'What about Lady Clandorris?' asked Deborah. 'She might catch you at the marsh pools.'

'Never!' said Samantha. 'I've never seen her go near the marsh pools at all. I believe what she said about taking the bogwoppits down there fifty times a day was just twaddle. Nobody has ever seen her there or they would have said so.'

They took one further precaution.

'Dad,' Jeff said, 'Samantha and me are going to take the bogwoppit back to the marsh pools.'

'That's a good job!' said Mr Price.

'But Dad,' said Jeff, 'can we stick something down the drain to prevent Lady Clandorris putting more disinfectant into the pools and killing it?'

'Disinfectant hadn't ought to be able to get into the pools at all,' said Mr Price, thinking aloud. 'The drain what she puts the disinfectant into goes into the main drain – joins it somewhere this side of the Park. There must be a leak to get it coming up in the pools, like. Now the secondary drain, what branches off the rest, that's as high and dry as a badger's nest. Nothing can't get in there, short of a flood. It hasn't been used for years. It's a regular beauty, as big as a palace, more like a cellar than a drain. Why, a man can stand upright in it! A little damp, but not dusty. Your bogwoppit wouldn't hurt in there.'

'Well, couldn't you block off the other part?' the children asked hopefully.

'What? Go up to the Park again? Not likely! When her Ladyship paid me for the grid she created something shocking, and said more or less that I was rooking her. I'm doing no more work for *her*!' said Mr Price. 'Not even if she asks me I won't, and catch me chasing *her* for a job!'

'The bogwoppit may die!' said Samantha. 'And it's the One-and-Only-Bogwoppit-in-the-World.'

'And the world's a better place for that!' said Mr Price with feeling. 'Even if you are right about it, my dear! I haven't seen the TV cameras rushing to take its picture yet!'

The children carried out their plan. Deborah and Tim circled the Park and saw through the windows of his cottage the gamekeeper and his wife watching Saturday sport on television. The dogs were shut up in pens, sleeping in the sun.

Climbing the Park gates at the back entrance, they waved handkerchiefs in the direction of the housing estate, where Samantha and Jeff, on the look-out, saw the small, white distant signals, and climbed over the railings of the Park, carrying the bogwoppit in the toolbag.

Samantha's heart ached at parting with it, though Jeff had promised to give her a piebald guinea pig to take its place. Secretly she felt certain that the bogwoppit would not leave her. Somehow or other she believed it would find her again, and she refused to face the question of what was to be done with it if it did.

To their relief, all over the borders of the marsh pools small clumps of aruncus wopitus were springing into life, apparently as prolific and as vigorous as before. Samantha picked some leaves and pulled up a couple of plants, just in case. They came more easily out of the bog than from the untended clay of Lady Clandorris's herb garden.

After a final hug she put the bogwoppit on the ground.

'I'm sorry!' she whispered, 'I'm terribly sorry! I wanted you to live with me, but . . .'

She expected the bogwoppit to cling to her knees, to sob and cry, to fly back into her arms. She fully believed it would refuse to go into the marsh pool without her. She thought she would have to push it away and run.

But the ungrateful little creature did not give her so much as a final glance. Spreading its ridiculous whirring wings it rose spinning into the air and dropped with a plop! into the middle of the marsh pool, spattering Samantha from head to foot with mud.

For a brief moment the top of its head reappeared, and she thought she saw its round eyes glistening just below the surface of the water. Then it vanished from sight, and presently the last bubble rose and burst, the last ripple from its plunging reached the shore and died away. The marsh pool became perfectly still.

'Great!' said Jeff with satisfaction.

Tears rolled slowly down Samantha's cheeks.

When he saw her distress Jeff tried to distract her.

'I wonder where that drain leaks?' he said. They explored the grass on the house side of the marsh pools, but there was nothing to give them any clue, and meanwhile the bogwoppit remained in terrible danger. Samantha could only hope that it would not betray itself to her Aunt Daisy by any unusual activity, or by battering too fiercely on the grid that Mr Price had made. But she knew just how noisy a noise it could make when it was bored or lonely.

She returned to the Prices feeling heavy-hearted, and Mrs Price was sorry for her missing her pet. She thought Samantha had had a hard deal in one way and another. 'Would you like to take over feeding Bill Budgie, love?' she offered. 'He always whistles for you!'

But long before bedtime Samantha had something quite different to occupy her mind, for Deborah crept up to her, ashen-faced, and whispered in her ear:

'You know those tadpoles the twins and I got that first time we went to the marsh pools? They've been all this time in the goldfish pond, and now they've just hatched. And they're none of them tadpoles at all. They're all bogwoppits!'

12. Tadpoles or Worse

SAMANTHA raced into the garden with Deborah beside her.

Beside the goldfish pond the twins were staring speechlessly at the seething mass of tiny bodies in the water below, where a hundred baby bogwoppits, infinitely small, were busily shedding the protective jelly that encased them and taking their first swim, frantically searching for food.

Thankful that they had brought back those few precious leaves from the marsh pools, Samantha began feverishly to shred them with her nail scissors. As she threw them into the goldfish pond the little creatures seized them avidly, three or four to every fragment. They seemed to be born with enormous appetites, and the water was alive with them. The goldfish, terrified, huddled under the waterlily leaves. One could almost see them trembling.

The children dared not linger long beside the pond for fear of attracting attention. The last thing they wanted was for Mr and Mrs Price to discover the newly-hatched bogwoppits.

The children's parents were in the habit of sitting out in the garden on a fine evening when the day's work was done, and when in spite of all their hopes it failed to rain on that particular evening Jeff and Timothy thoughtfully placed chairs for their father and mother in a corner well away from the pond, arranging them with their backs towards the teeming, tearing surface of the water.

When darkness fell they breathed more easily. A subdued whimpering and squeaking arose from the goldfish pond, but passed for the twittering of drowsy birds.

Everybody went to bed.

In the morning the pond was not nearly so lively. The baby bogwoppits had grown a little, and the jelly had all disappeared. But they looked weak and flabby, unhealthy and subdued, lying about in opposite corners to the goldfish, which looked even more dejected than the bogwoppits.

Samantha shredded more leaves into the water, but the little creatures nibbled them listlessly.

'It's drains they want!' said Samantha. 'It isn't natural for them living in a place like this! We have got to get them back to the marsh pools!'

The bogwoppits seemed doomed in all possible directions. If Mr Price saw them in such amazing quantities he would be bound to put them into a bucket of disinfectant, while up in the marsh pools they risked a similar fate at the hands of Lady Clandorris. The only hope was that they would keep to their own part of the drain and she would never discover how many of them were living on the wrong side of the grid. But it all seemed very unlikely.

'We'll take them up after dark, tonight!' Samantha said. 'It ought to be as safe as houses then.'

But in the meantime the baby bogwoppits died in their dozens. Jeff reported many floating on the surface at eleven o'clock. 'And a goldfish!' Tim said sullenly. The goldfish were his.

Frantically Samantha shredded aruncus wopitus into even smaller pieces, but it lay floating idly on the surface of the water. Another goldfish ate some and died. And the plants Samantha had brought out of the marsh pools had not survived in Mrs Price's flower border. Already they had turned a sickly yellow colour, spreading decaying leaves across the soil of the flower bed.

'They will soon all be dead!' said Deborah sorrowfully.

'*And* all my goldfish!' added Timothy with resentment.

'They ought to be put in the marsh pools *now*!' said Samantha.

'Yes they ought!' all the others agreed.

'We had better take them at once!' said Samantha.

Relieved that she had made a definite decision the twins began to bail bogwoppits out of the pond with a bucket, while Deborah fetched her father's toolbag. They emptied bogwoppits into the bag and removed goldfish back into the water until at last it seemed as if everything was where it was intended to be. There was enough water slopping about inside the bag to keep the baby bogwoppits alive, if not happy.

As it was Sunday afternoon they all hoped the keeper would be off duty, added to which the success of the previous expedition had made them braver.

With Samantha carrying the bogwoppits, the four of them left Mr and Mrs Price watching telly and climbed over the railings into the Park.

'It's leaking terribly!' Samantha said as water splashed on her jeans and ran down into her shoes. 'There can't be an awful lot left inside it!'

They stopped to look, and she was perfectly right, because at the bottom of the toolbag the baby bogwoppits lay thrashing about in a welter of wet and wriggling bodies, some of which lay ominously still.

'We were so stupid not to bring some mud!' said Samantha. 'We could have mixed it up out of the flower beds. Now they may all die before they get there. Come on, let's run!'

But they had hardly closed the toolbag before Deborah stopped short in her tracks uttering a shriek. In the not so far distance they could all hear the sound of loud barking across the Park, and out of the woods strode Lady Clandorris's keeper, who had already unleashed his two large dogs, which, uttering horribly fierce and threatening noises, were bearing down upon the children as fast as they could gallop.

Deborah turned tail and scurried for the Park palings. She reached them and sat on the top rail trembling and crying as she expected Samantha and the boys to be eaten up in front of her eyes.

Samantha would have run too, but she was hampered by the bag of wet bogwoppits, which was not light, due to the wet canvas and all the pond water running through it. Also, they were not a great distance from the marsh pools, and she wanted to empty out the precious cargo before the keeper reached them. In spite of her very real fear of the dogs she had her pride. She still regarded herself as belonging to the Park, even if living in exile. Lady Clandorris was still her Aunt Daisy, and if she could prevent it she was not going to flee for her life in front of her Aunt Daisy's gamekeeper.

So she waved her arm furiously and shouted across the Park:

'Call your dogs off! Stop them! Stop them at once! Make them go away!'

Jeff and Timothy had followed Deborah for a few paces only, terrified of the keeper and his dogs but unwilling to desert Samantha. They thought she was quite crazy to defy the man in such a reckless manner, but they hesitated, just to see what would happen. After all, they were closer to the fence than they were to the keeper.

Samantha was actually advancing, and to their surprise and admiration they saw that the angry dogs had stopped on the far side of the pools, and were barking loudly across the water. Their heads were held low and their hackles were bristling.

Samantha took a few paces forward and the dogs became even more furious. It was rather like a game of Grandmother's Steps with the grandmother never turning her back but always looking at you.

The keeper was approaching fast. Contrary to Samantha's order he seemed to be urging his dogs on from a distance. The children could hear his exhortations to 'See 'em off, boys! Just see 'em off!'

The dogs grew braver as their master came up behind them. They bounded forward, splashing into the pools which was the quickest way to reach the children. Samantha had reached the pools too, but she was frightened, and now for the first time she began to retreat. As the dogs came on so she retreated, and the twins were quite prepared to see her drop the toolbag and break into a run, when something happened.

The dogs were bounding through the mud and water, barking at the same time and making great leaps that landed them now in deeper and now in more shallow water.

Suddenly, just in front of their noses and loudly snapping jaws, something rose like a bullet out of the mud, screaming and chattering and flailing its small wings. It was the bogwoppit.

The dogs stopped short in their tracks. Their barking turned to uneasy growls as the mud and water streamed off their heaving sides. With a howl they pulled themselves out of the pools, turned tail and fled towards their master, still whimpering, and slavering at the mouth in fear and disgust.

'Bogwoppit!' cried Samantha.

The bogwoppit flopped and flapped towards her, then rose head high in its spinning flight, and dropped like a wet fruit on her shoulder, where it smothered her head and neck in muddy kisses. Then it crashed back into the pool and disappeared, while Samantha, looking calmer and more collected than she felt, emptied the contents of the toolbag under the very eyes of the keeper, who now arrived on the far side of the pools to challenge her.

'And what may you be doing here?' he said disagreeably. He had been very shaken by the behaviour of his dogs, and thought the children must have ill-treated them.

'Tadpoles!' said Samantha, firmly shaking out the bag among the half-submerged roots of aruncus wopitus.

'And I guess you rightly know you are not allowed to come trespassing in this Park!' the keeper said warningly.

'Lady Clandorris is my aunt!' said Samantha coldly. The keeper looked interested.

'Oh, you are that one, are you?' he said reluctantly. 'Well, who are all those others then?'

'Those are my friends,' said Samantha, looking towards the retreating Prices, who, now that Samantha seemed to be in charge of the situation, were walking fast and in a dignified fashion towards the fence.

'Well, Lady Clandorris doesn't want children coming into the Park!' said the gamekeeper. 'And that's the orders she has given me. "You keep 'em out of the Park!" she tells me. "Or else".'

'You had no business to set your dogs on children,' Samantha said. 'Did my aunt tell you to do that, too?'

'They wouldn't hurt anybody. It's all just row with them,' said the gamekeeper. 'What did you do to them anyway, to make them run away like that? Did you throw something at them?'

'No, of course I didn't!' Samantha retorted. 'They just don't happen to like tadpoles, that's all.'

The keeper looked at her with suspicion, tinged with respect.

'Well if your aunt told you to bring children in the Park she never told *me*!' he said, turning away. 'I'll have it out with her in the morning. I mean, it can't be one thing one day and another the next! I'll have to see what she wants me to do about it. I can't be monkeyed about like this.'

'Just as you like!' said Samantha. Her mission being accomplished she joined the Prices, while the keeper, still grumbling, made his way home across the Park.

Samantha looked back, just once. Not at the keeper, but at the marsh pools. She hoped to see the not-quite-One-and-Only-Bogwoppit-in-the-World holding out its wings to her, or at least peering after her as if it cared. But no head of frowsty feathers, no round eyes appeared above the surface of the pools. Instead, the water was feverish with dancing, darting, delirious baby bogwoppits, hurtling about among the leaves of aruncus wopitus, so that from where she stood anyone might have thought the water was being whipped and tormented by the frenzy of a summer storm.

13. The Disappearance of
Lady Clandorris

'I SAW your auntie in the town on Saturday!' Miss Mellor said to Samantha on Monday morning. 'Now I really would like to begin a Project on those little rare animals we were talking about. Have you still got yours?'

'No,' said Samantha. 'It's back in the marsh pools.'

'Ah!' said Miss Mellor. 'Well, that will be still more interesting, because we can study all its natural ways and habits. Will you ask your auntie if it is all right for us to go into the Park one afternoon?'

'I don't see her nowadays,' said Samantha. 'I'm staying with the Prices.'

Miss Mellor looked puzzled.

'Don't you see your auntie sometimes?' she asked in surprise.

'Not ever,' said Samantha flatly.

'Then perhaps I had better ask her myself,' said Miss Mellor. 'I will write her a note.'

'She doesn't read notes. Or letters,' said Samantha. 'She leaves them lying in the letter box for weeks and weeks. Nobody ever looks at them.'

'Oh dear!' said Miss Mellor. There was a long silence.

Samantha spoke first.

'If we found things out about the bogwoppit, would the television people come and photograph it?' she asked.

'I should think that is quite likely ... if it really *is* a bogwoppit!' said Miss Mellor. 'Almost everybody is bound to be interested.'

'Would it be *conserved*?' asked Samantha.

'Oh yes!' Miss Mellor said. 'The moment I find out that it is really what we think it is I shall write to the Society for the Protection of Rare and Rural Life, and there is no doubt at all that it will be given strict protection.'

'Nobody would be allowed to kill it for any reason at all?' pursued Samantha.

'Most certainly not!' said Miss Mellor very emphatically. 'Once it is proclaimed a protected animal, or bird, or whatever it calls itself, it will be a crime to harm it in any way at all.'

'Good!' said Samantha in great relief. 'Do you mean they would be punished by law if they hurt it?'

'Yes I do!' Miss Mellor assured her.

'Well then, I'll ask Aunt Daisy,' said Samantha.

'Of course, passing a protection order isn't done all at once ... it would probably have to go through Parliament,' said Miss Mellor.

'Then we had better hurry up!' said Samantha.

She wrote a letter to Lady Clandorris in class, and decided to ask Ozzy Wallace to ask his father to deliver it with the milk. At the same time she remembered her own decision never to speak to her aunt again, but after all, a letter was different to a conversation. She was not at all confident of success, but she wrote the letter just the same.

Dear Aunt Daisy Clandorris,

I hope you are well. My class would like to go into the Park to study the habits of the bogwoppits that you killed in the marsh pools. It is a crime to kill rare and innocent animals like bogwoppits and this is to be an act of Parliament in future punished by the laws of our land. I hope you will say yes to

my teacher Miss Mellor and give the answer
to the milkman Mr Wallace.

Yours sincerely,

Samantha

Ozzy Wallace assured Samantha that he
had given the note to his father to deliver to
Lady Clandorris in the morning. Samantha
had not enclosed it in an envelope so that it
would be easier to read, and there would be
no excuse for Lady Clandorris to leave it
unopened. On Wednesday morning Ozzy told
Samantha that his father had delivered it into
her aunt's hands, but no answer came.

Samantha wrote the letter again, word for
word, and again Ozzy's father took it up to
the Park. When still no answer came Samantha
wrote it out for a third time, in block letters,
using a felt-tipped pen. She asked the milkman
herself to leave it wide open on the doorstep.

The next evening Ozzy brought her an
answer which his father had collected in the

morning. It consisted of her three letters pinned together, and across each letter in large black capitals was scrawled the word 'NO!'

Ozzy did not repeat his father's comment, which was that both Samantha and her aunt were round the bend.

To Miss Mellor, Samantha worded her aunt's refusal rather differently. She explained that her aunt did not want any of them in the Park just at present. It was something to do with the drains, she said.

Miss Mellor at once agreed that if there was any doubt about the drains it was much better to wait for a while. 'Perhaps later in the summer!' she suggested.

Samantha went across the Park in the dusk to have a look at the bogwoppits. She only caught a brief glimpse of about half a dozen, but these were already half grown. She had not realized that they could develop so fast. And to her hidden shame she had to admit that they all looked very alike. It was extremely difficult to tell them apart from her own especial One-and-Only-Bogwoppit. None of them came out to greet her. They seemed very much wilder and less tame than the original bogwoppits, sinking below the surface of the water and eyeing her suspiciously from between the aruncus wopitus leaves, with their round, blue, limpid eyes.

The Prices had other things to think about . . . sports and athletics, a school excursion to the sea, and a school camp in Wales. Samantha was good at sport and enjoyed camping, but she thought all the time of the bogwoppits and the Park, and the stately home that ought to have been hers if Lady Clandorris had been a more natural aunt. Not that she wasn't happy with the Prices, which was as good a home as anybody could wish for, but it just didn't happen to be hers.

Her Aunt Lily had written again from America to say that Duggie had lost his job and they couldn't have Samantha after all. This letter too lay in the hall letter box up at the Park, and nobody read it or was any the wiser. America was such a long way away.

To maintain the impression that she did in fact belong to the place, Samantha walked round the outside of the Park nearly every evening. She was bound to meet the keeper on one of these perambulations, and she did, but she was not trespassing, so he did not attempt to loose his dogs, who looked quite amicable on their leashes, walking beside him.

Samantha did not expect the keeper to stop and talk to her, unless he meant to tick her off, and she was walking past with her head in the air when to her surprise he said to her:

'How's your auntie then?'

Samantha stopped and stared. The keeper was much more likely to know the state of Lady Clandorris's health than she was herself.

'She's all right!' she said haughtily, not wishing to start a conversation with the keeper. They went their different ways.

A few days later she met him again.

'Where's your auntie?' he asked her this time.

Samantha was unprepared for this.

'I don't know!' she said defensively.

'You don't know?' he demanded. 'You don't live at the Park any more then? I never did think you belonged to her. She's not your real auntie, is she?'

'She *is* my real auntie, and I *do* belong to the Park!' Samantha said indignantly. 'I'm just staying with the Prices at present, that's all!'

'Oh you are, are you?' said the gamekeeper. 'Well, it's over a week since I saw your auntie and she owes me three weeks' wages.'

Samantha looked supercilious.

'Well I can't do anything about that, can I?' she said. 'I expect she will come back and pay you tomorrow.'

'She'd better, or she'll lose I,' said the keeper angrily. He walked away grumbling.

Samantha wondered whether she would walk back across the Park, under the very window of the house, and then decided against it. Her Aunt Daisy might be there all the time, with a cold or something, and Samantha did not want to be routed for a second time, or she might even say, for a third.

But Ozzy Wallace told her in the morning that the milk bottles had not been taken in for several days.

'My dad says she has done it before,' Ozzy said. 'Just gone away and never told him, and made ever such a fuss when she came back and found all that milk had gone bad.'

'Tell him not to leave any more!' said Samantha. 'Tell him I said so!'

Ozzy's father left no more milk, but he called at the Park in the mornings just in case there was an order. The order never came, and no empty milk bottles were put outside. He took the sour milk bottles away again.

'My dad says you ought to go up to the Park and see about your auntie!' Ozzy Wallace told Samantha. 'He's knocked and knocked and knocked, and nobody comes, and he went round the back and saw her ladyship's car in the garage. He thinks she may be ill.'

For caution's sake Samantha went round the Park to tell the keeper of Mr Wallace's suspicions. But the keeper was loading all his furniture on a van and leaving that very night.

'Four week's wages she owes me now!' he told Samantha. 'I'm not stopping. She did it once before, and I told her next time would be the last.'

'Mr Wallace the milkman thinks she may be ill,' said Samantha.

'Then you'd better fetch an ambulance,' said the keeper unsympathetically. He whistled his dogs into the back of the van and drove away.

Samantha felt very deserted and almost helpless. She did not like the keeper but he was a part of the Park and a link with her aunt, Lady Clandorris. She really did not know what to do next.

Reluctantly she left the keeper's cottage and entered the back gates of the Park. She began to walk slowly towards the house.

It had always been the quietest and most deserted house she had ever known, so it was not surprising that there should be no sign of life anywhere around it. And it felt more empty than she had ever known it to feel, even before she went inside it. In fact the memories of her last visit were still so vivid that it took all her courage to mount the steps and knock on the front door, after she had walked round the outside of the house two or three times, half dreading and half hoping to see her aunt's head come popping out of one of the upstairs windows. She would not even had objected to dodging a bucket of disinfectant as a proof of Lady Clandorris being alive and healthy.

But when absolutely nothing happened, and no reply came from her knocking, she gave the door a push, and found that it was not locked but opened quite easily. Samantha entered a completely empty hall.

No crumpets today. No glowing fire in the grate. Only the pheasant feather hat was there as before, lying on a chair. It looked as if it had lain there for years and years.

'So she's not out!' thought Samantha, with a shiver of apprehension. She waited and listened. There was no sound in the house at all.

Slowly it came to her that perhaps Ozzy's father had been right. Aunt Daisy might be lying upstairs ill! Ill and helpless, unable to make anyone hear her ... why! she might have been lying there for days!

And as this possibility grew larger and more likely the thought came into Samantha's mind that here, perhaps was her opportunity at last! Now, after long weeks, Lady Clandorris would at last be pleased – *thankful* – to see her only niece arrived to save her, and Samantha would forgive all and nurse her back to life. Fantastic pictures began to spin in Samantha's brain as she imagined Aunt Daisy convalescent, leaning on her shoulder for support, fumbling her way about the Park with a stick, and telling her niece that from now on they must always make their home together.

And thinking these beautiful thoughts Samantha began very slowly to climb the stairs.

14. Alone in the House

HALFWAY up the stairs the dream vanished, while a much more sinister vision took its place.

Suppose Aunt Daisy were not ill but – dead?

Samantha came to a sudden halt. She felt she simply could not face finding a dead person all by herself. She decided to go home and fetch the Prices.

But as she turned to descend she stopped again. Because if Lady Clandorris were not dead but very, very ill there was no time to be lost, and she ought to fetch a doctor as quickly as possible. Slowly she began to creep back up the stairs.

On the landing she stopped, listening for a groan. None came. There was no sound in the house except for Samantha's nervous breathing.

She was so anxious now that she ventured to call: 'Aunt Daisy!' almost under her breath, and then a little louder. It sounded like a shout in the dreadful silence. There was no answer.

Terrified now, Samantha moved on towards Lady Clandorris's bedroom door, dragging her feet and clinging to the wall with both hands as if it could shelter her. It seemed a mile and a half along the corridor to Aunt Daisy's bedroom, and when she got there the door was shut.

Samantha's fingers closed round the chipped china handle. She almost longed to find it locked, but it turned, creaking, as almost everything creaked in the old house when it was interfered with. She stood holding the door an eighth of an inch ajar, and not daring to look inside.

But having gone so far the job had to be finished, so opening the door a fraction wider, Samantha put her eye to the chink and peered inside the bedroom.

The complete emptiness of the bedroom surged out to meet her. It was almost like having a slap in the face. Slowly Samantha went inside to meet it.

There was nobody there at all. The bed was made, Aunt Daisy's worn hairbrush lay on the dressing table. Her coat was on the back of a chair, and her tattered dressing gown hung on a peg. On one side of the cracked looking glass dangled her bunch of keys. But of Lady Clandorris there was not a sign.

'She *has* gone away!' thought Samantha in relief. And then she thought of the car in the garage, of the hat in the hall, and of Aunt Daisy's coat, hanging here on a peg under her very eyes. Where would she go without her hat, her coat, her car and her bunch of keys? Perhaps she has been taken ill somewhere else in the house, thought Samantha. She went upstairs to the landing above, where her old, empty bedroom received her coldly.

Nowhere was there any sign of her aunt. She explored the house from top to bottom, and then, feeling that here was a mystery too big for her to tackle alone, she went back to tell the Prices.

Deborah, Jeff and Timothy received the news with incredulity. When they were certain that Samantha was not telling them some imaginary story they wanted to set out for the Park at once, to see for themselves this remarkable act of disappearance. They were all certain that Samantha must have overlooked some vital clue that would tell them exactly where Lady Clandorris was.

They agreed not to tell their parents for the moment. In next to no time the police would be involved, besides which Deborah, Jeff and Timothy longed for the delicious privilege of exploring the house again from top to bottom, without fear of the keeper, and with the very real prospect of unravelling a mystery.

They were not quite so brave when they arrived at the Park, but the open front door, the immense quiet and Samantha's confidence drew them on. They went from room to room, even looking inside the cupboards, 'In case she has been murdered!' said Jeff with determination. Their courage rose as it became quite obvious that they had the house to themselves. Tim searched the herb garden, which looked quite different by evening light, and not at all alarming. But Lady Clandorris was not to be found among the herbs, although they searched every inch of the little patch where they had previously hidden.

There was a half-eaten meal on the kitchen table, but as Lady Clandorris seldom cleared up after herself, sometimes leaving her dirty plates about for days, Samantha did not think this was very peculiar or unusual. Neither did the untidiness of the store cupboard shock her, though the contents were spilling all over the shelves. But Lady Clandorris never put anything neatly away.

Samantha had looked inside the cellar, but now she looked again, with the Prices to support her. They all climbed down the steps into the damp, dark room that gave entry to the big drain that had once been used by the bogwoppits.

The last time she had visited it the drain shaft had smelled strongly of disinfectant, but now that particular smell was quite gone, and the earthy, marshy boggy odour was once more apparent.

'Pooh! The bogwoppits don't half pong!' said Timothy. 'And all that way off too! The marsh pool must be miles away, and so is my dad's grid.'

'He locked it!' said Jeff. 'So they can't get up here any more, but they do pong all right!'

Close to the entrance to the drain shaft were two full buckets of disinfectant standing ready for use. Samantha carried them up the steps and emptied them down the sink. When she returned with the empty buckets the twins were peering into the old drain.

'It's like a secret passage!' they said. 'Shall we go down and look at the grid our Dad made?'

'It's filthy dirty!' said Deborah. 'You'll catch it from Mum if you go down there. She said your shirts had got to see tomorrow out, and you'll only get all mucky down that place. I'm not going!'

'I would if I had a torch!' said Jeff.

'We ought to go home,' said Deborah.

'I'm not going home!' said Samantha. She never knew what suddenly made her so brave. 'If my aunt is away there ought to be somebody looking after the place while she's gone. I belong to it and I'm going to stay here.'

She actually felt a responsibility for the big old empty house, and the thought of being in complete charge of it made her forget the long, dark lonely hours ahead. She had never been afraid of the house itself, only of Lady Clandorris and her rages.

'I'll stay with you!' Jeff said at once.

Deborah looked doubtful.

'What shall I tell Mum and Dad?' she said.

'Say me and Sam are staying the night at the Park!' Jeff retorted.

'They'll ask ever such a lot of questions!' said Deborah.

'You go home then!' Samantha told him. 'It won't look so funny if I stay alone. You come up in the morning. There's no school. We can spend the weekend here. You can say I stayed to see my auntie come home!'

Reluctantly the Prices left her.

*

Samantha felt proud and independent. It was such a long time since she had been alone by herself anywhere, and the solitude was quite a relief. She went into the pianola room and began to play all her favourite tunes one after the other.

When she returned to the hall it smelled of bogwoppits.

'Ugh!' said Samantha aloud. The Prices had left the cellar door open. When she went to shut it the cellar steps seemed very damp. 'I hope there isn't going to be a flood!' thought Samantha.

She went to the store cupboard to find some food for herself, and discovered that the shelves were nearly empty. This was peculiar because Lady Clandorris always kept her shelves so well stocked that there was enough food to last her a lifetime, Samantha had considered in the days when she was a visitor at the Park. And now nearly all the food was gone.

Her first suspicions fell on the gamekeeper. Perhaps he knew all the time that Lady Clandorris was not in the house, and had stolen the food in place of the wages she owed him? But Samantha had seen the inside of the van when he left his cottage, and there had been no sign of the stacks and stacks of tins and boxes he would have had to take with him if he had robbed Lady Clandorris's cupboards.

Whoever the robber might be, he had taken advantage of Lady Clandorris's disappearance to help himself, and suddenly Samantha began to feel less confident. A moment ago the empty house seemed to belong to her, and to herself alone, but now there was the possibility of sharing it with a burglar, and this was not at all a pleasant thought. She turned from the cupboard trembling, and almost screamed aloud as something moved in the shadow behind her.

Something was crouching in the arch of the entrance to the great drain, and it now emerged, looking at her defiantly, and, she thought, with malice. It was followed by another shadow, and yet another.

Three, four, five bogwoppits marched out of the drain, slopping with wet feet across the cellar floor to the store cupboard.

Infinitely relieved that it was only bogwoppits and nothing human, Samantha held out her arms to them, but the little creatures ignored her. Each in turn spread its wings and made its whirring ascent to the shelves above its head. With eager wing and claw it took possession of the remaining provisions. Then each bogwoppit dropped to the floor, and pushed, rolled and chivvied its booty into the entrance of the drain, before trundling it out of sight into the darkness beyond.

When she realized what was happening Samantha sprang to protect her Aunt Daisy's property. She was horrified by the barefaced pilfering, on such a gigantic scale, by the bogwoppits. They must have been at it for days. And how had they penetrated Mr Price's grid? He had been so convinced it was 'rat-proof', and strong enough to resist them. But bogwoppits penetrate anything.

Samantha rushed upstairs to fetch the store cupboard key from her Aunt Daisy's bedroom, but it was gone. There were only the car keys left, and the big key that locked the front door. But there were a great many muddy footprints round the room, and some of them were on the bed.

When she returned to the kitchen a second lot of bogwoppits had arrived. They were more determined – if anything – than the last.

'You can't do that! You mustn't take things away!' Samantha cried, standing in front of the cupboard with her arms spread wide to prevent them from reaching the shelves. 'You must leave her some food! You can't steal just everything!'

The bogwoppits reply was to rush past her towards the cupboard. In a moment Samantha was the centre of flailing wings and wet, scratching feet. She pushed them away but she was no match for such an army of them. They simply knocked her down and helped themselves to what they wanted. When they had emptied the shelves of the remaining stores, they bundled them away, whistling and hooting impishly at her as they vanished into the drain. Samantha might never have existed for them. She could hear them singing for a long time, and then, far off down the tunnel something clanged dully, like a gate.

'It must be Mr Price's grid, and they've got the key!' thought Samantha, looking at the completely empty cupboards and the bogwoppits' dirty footmarks trailing across the cellar floor.

Suddenly with all her heart and soul she detested bogwoppits.

15. A Question of a Ransom

SAMANTHA closed and bolted the door to the cellar.

She was on the point of abandoning the house and going back to the Prices, but a feeling stronger than her fear and distaste prevented her from leaving. It was an odd kind of loyalty to the Park, and an unwillingness to leave it to be overrun and pillaged by the little monsters belonging to the underworld of the drains below. She walked as far as the front door, and then quite firmly shut and locked it, before walking calmly upstairs to her bedroom on the second floor. The bric-a-brac and pieces of furniture she had selected to live with greeted her like old friends.

Unashamedly she pulled a chest of drawers across the door and went to bed. She did not hear a sound the whole night long.

In the morning the cellar was dry and deserted, but Samantha was running no risks. She filled the buckets with a new mixture of disinfectant and stood them on either side of the entrance to the old drain. And just for good measure she slopped a little on the ground and watched it trickle away into the darkness – not enough to travel far, but she hoped it would convey a positive message.

Instead, as she sat down to eat the only food left in the house, a half bowl of stale cereals without milk or sugar, a pitiful sound arose in the cellar below, a mewing and a sobbing and a wailing that was so familiar she did not hesitate to thrust the cereal aside as she rushed down the cellar stairs to meet it.

Out of the drain emerged a bogwoppit, shuffling and crying, splashed with disinfectant and wailing loudly. It paused to be sick, and then with its last feeble strength, rose desperately into the air, and flew, damp, sodden and wretched, straight into Samantha's arms.

Although there was little to distinguish it from any of the newly hatched bogwoppits that had recently invaded the house, Samantha knew without a shadow of doubt that this one must be, had to be, in fact *was* ... the Only-Bogwoppit-in-the-World, come back to visit her.

The bogwoppit shivered violently, vibrating like a small engine. It pecked at its sodden feathers, and shook its disinfected feet. Finally it flopped out of her arms and led the way up the stairs to the bathroom still shivering and sobbing.

There was no hot water, but the little creature did not seem to notice. Only when it was standing in the water flapping its ridiculous little wings with pleasure did Samantha notice something white sticking out of its feathers.

Whatever it was fell suddenly into the water, and the bogwoppit trod on it. By the time Samantha had rescued it and found that it was a square-shaped piece of paper with writing on it, the ink had run, and it was extremely difficult to decipher what it was all about.

When Samantha did manage to read the note her face turned very pale indeed, and her hands began to tremble.

The Prices, arriving in the hall below, shouted her name and pounded up the stairs to the second floor landing. They found Samantha still holding the piece of paper and staring at it, while the bogwoppit stood on its head on the plughole.

'They've got her!' Samantha said hoarsely. 'The bogwoppits have got my aunt, Lady

Clandorris, down the drain. And they are keeping her a prisoner.'

'NO!' exclaimed all three Prices.

'Look at this!' said Samantha. The Prices looked.

The message was very faint, having been in the bath with the bogwoppit.

It said:

TELL SAMANTHA THE
BOGWOPPITS HAVE GOT ME
DOWN THE DRAIN.
Daisy Clandorris.

Even in her horror and dismay Samantha's heart throbbed for a moment as she realized that at last her aunt had recognized her existence, and had even voiced a kind of plea for her help. Samantha was ready to offer that help to the utmost of her ability.

She led the way at a gallop down the stairs, followed by the three Prices, also the bogwoppit, who was dragging a towel and uttering shrieks of pleasure at the thought of finding some cobwebs to roll in.

The drain was dark and damp. Nobody had a torch. When they tried to enter the drain the bogwoppit gibbered and flapped at them. It could only be pacified in Samantha's arms, wrapped up like a baby in the wet towel. She told Jeff where to find a small hand torch that was in a drawer in the kitchen, and with this most inadequate light and fiercely beating hearts they stepped into the drain.

Samantha's chief fear was of being rushed again by bogwoppits in the dark, but it was Deborah who was the most anxious of the four of them. She hung back, while Samantha with great courage took the lead, carrying the torch. The bogwoppit struggled in her arms, longing to get down and rub itself against the dirty walls of the drain. It only enjoyed a bath for the pleasure of getting filthy again.

Samantha did not want to let it escape because it still seemed to love her, and she hoped it would persuade the other bogwoppits to be friends with her. So she petted it and soothed it, holding it very firmly in the towel, which it began to rip to pieces.

Sooner than they had expected the faint light of the torch showed up the bars of the grid that Mr Price had made, and sure enough, the gate in it stood open. It looked as if Lady Clandorris might have penetrated the drain as far as the grid, unlocked the door and been captured in the passage. The feeble light lit up a shoe lying on the far side of the grid, while beads were scattered so widely about the floor that one or the other of them was constantly treading them underfoot.

As they stood uncertain beside the open gate, the drain, like a long and evil snake, stretched ahead of them, and suddenly there came the unmistakable sound of action at the farther end, moans, twitters, chattering bogwoppit noises to which none of them were strangers. There came the damp slapping of feet on wet earth, the rustling of many moist feathery wings, and the unmistakable threat in the darkness of something unknown, and possibly unfriendly, that brought them to a halt as they wondered how to proceed.

At the same time the One-and-Only-Bogwoppit, having torn the towel to pieces, made one tremendous leap out of Samantha's arms into the drain, and galloped out of sight without so much as a backward glance.

The advancing noise grew louder and more menacing. Suddenly the shrieks became piercing as the One-and-Only joined forces with its friends and poured no one knew what exaggerated stories into their ears.

'Shut the gate!' shrieked Deborah, for Samantha seemed paralysed. She was stunned by the bogwoppit's desertion. It had seemed so devoted and so glad to be with her again.

The boys rushed at the grill and dragged at the gate till it closed. Mechanically Samantha turned and pocketed the key. The next moment a score of black and furry bodies hurled themselves against the bars, screeching, chattering and thrusting forward their small black wings as their beaks attacked the grill. But Mr Price's handiwork was too much for them and they drew back, staring inquisitively at the children out of the darkness with their round blue eyes, that gleamed in the beam of Samantha's light. She tried in vain to distinguish the beloved features of the One-and-Only, but not a single bogwoppit responded to her advances. From each pair of eyes came the same distrustful stare, and when she approached the grid they got frightened and snapped at her.

'Oh do bring the torch! It's so *dark*!' Deborah pleaded, already halfway up the tunnel to the house.

Samantha turned and followed.

'Hang on to the key!' Jeff warned her.

It was good to see the daylight again. They faced one another in the cellar and recognized the same tenseness in each face.

'Do you think Lady Clandorris is still alive down there?' Tim said. 'They might have killed her! Or she might have starved to death!'

'She wrote the message herself,' said Samantha. 'And the bogwoppits took all that food down the drain – masses and masses of it. Enough to keep her for years, I should think. They don't eat such things themselves, so they must have meant to feed her with them. But I haven't an idea how we are going to get her out or rescue her.'

'Easy!' said Jeff. 'Just slosh down a lot of disinfectant, like my dad did last time. That'll settle the bogwoppits, and if your auntie gets a bit wet she won't mind if it means her getting free.'

'I don't want the bogwoppits killed,' said Samantha slowly. She was still thinking of the One-and-Only, and strangely enough, of the black, furry, dirty, strangely lovable little bogwoppits themselves.

'Don't you want to save your auntie?' said the Prices, astonished.

'Not that way!' said Samantha. 'I'd much rather rescue her *and* have the bogwoppits, *and* have the Project, *and* go on telly. We might be able to pay a ransom for her.'

'How could we find out what kind of ransom they would want?' said Deborah.

'We'll ask,' said Samantha.

She wrote a message on a piece of paper, put it in a polythene bag, and marched down the passage to the grill quite by herself. She thrust it through the bars and sluiced it on its way with a pailful of perfectly ordinary tap water. The message was simply: 'DO THEY WANT A RANSOM? HOW MUCH?'

'You are brave!' shuddered Deborah when she returned. 'I wouldn't go down that drain again for a thousand pounds!'

'I think we ought to tell my father,' said Tim.

Samantha knew that if any grown-ups were brought into it the bogwoppits chances of survival were very slim. And another thought was emerging. It was one thing to be the heroine of Aunt Daisy's rescue, and quite another to have her reinstated as mistress of the Park. How long would her gratitude last? Would she now accept Samantha into her house as her rightful niece and heiress, or would she send her packing again, and merely seal off the drain for ever with cement? And if so, was it really worth all the trouble of pacifying the bogwoppits just to have things exactly the same as they had been before?

With Aunt Daisy a prisoner a whole vista of opportunities opened out before Samantha's eyes. There was the Project. There was the freedom of the Park. There was the distinction of being at last, if only temporarily, the sole mistress in charge of the house and property, to which she felt so strong a claim.

'How can she send back an answer if the gate is locked?' asked Deborah.

'They can push it through the bars. I shall go down and look every hour,' said Samantha. The Prices looked at her with respect. None of them fancied a return journey into the depths of the drain.

'I think we ought to tell my dad,' said Timothy.

'Not till we get an answer from my aunt,' said Samantha firmly. 'You know what will happen if the grown-ups rescue her. We'll never be allowed in this house again, nor in the Park, and none of us will ever get on telly. But if we rescue her ourselves we can do the Project and keep the bogwoppits too. We'll make it a condition.'

'But bogwoppits are awful!' Deborah shivered.

'Not the One-and-Only isn't,' said Samantha. 'And we might tame the others in time. They are all right in their own place. Just think! We may be able to come up to the house and play the pianola when we want to! My aunt will *have* to be grateful to us if we rescue her.'

At the end of an hour, and again at the end of a second, she went down the old drain to the grid, Jeff following to keep her company, but nobody came to push a message through the bars, and not a sound could be heard down the long, dark tunnel ahead. It curved away out of sight much farther than the beam of Samantha's torch could follow.

Meanwhile the Prices played the pianola to their hearts' content.

Finally it was time to go home to dinner.

'Don't say a word to anybody!' Samantha urged them as the four took a short cut across the once-forbidden Park.

'I do think we ought to tell my dad,' said Timothy.

'I thought you liked playing the pianola!' said Samantha severely. 'You can play it quite a lot more before we rescue her if you leave things to me, but if you tell your dad you'll never play it again, most likely.'

As they skirted the marsh pools, something white floating on the water caught their attention. It was a small sheet of paper, such as might be torn from a person's shopping list. It looked wet, but not sodden, in fact it did not seem to have been in the water for any length of time.

Jeff waded in over his ankles to get it, and distinctly saw the pale blue eyes of a bogwoppit sinking out of sight below the surface.

Samantha saw it too, and snatched the paper out of Jeff's hands. There were words running across the paper, and this time they were written in pencil, so had not been washed away by the water.

TRY TWO THOUSAND BLACK BEETLES, the words ran.

'Whatever does it mean?' asked Deborah.

'The ransom!' said Samantha. 'They want two thousand black beetles as a ransom for her. Poor Aunt Daisy!'

'That's a lot of black beetles!' said Tim anxiously.

'It will give us time!' said Samantha, thinking: she can't possibly expect us to produce those overnight. I never thought of beetles, but I do remember that the One-and-Only used to eat them when he found any. 'Now don't say a thing to anybody!' she repeated. 'We'll find out if she needs anything while we are collecting the ransom, and in the meantime – well! Just think of all the things we can do while we've got the Park to ourselves!'

After dinner they put a message into an old bottle and dropped it into the marsh pool. The message said: RANSOM UNDER WAY. DO YOU WANT ANYTHING? Almost immediately a head rose to the surface. A beak or a wing seized the bottle and bore it down to the murky depths under the duckweed.

Tim and Deborah watched the marsh pools for an answer while Samantha and Jeff visited the grid at regular intervals. The answer came back in the same bottle. It popped up in the middle of the pool while Deborah and Tim were watching aeroplanes. They ran up to the Park to give it to Samantha.

The message read:

I WANT TO BE FREE. TRY TWO THOUSAND BLACK BEETLES.

'We *are* trying two thousand black beetles!' Samantha grumbled. She had caught three inside the drain, but having nothing to contain them in had lost them almost as fast.

They spent the rest of the afternoon looking in the cupboards and dark and dusty places, but it was evident that two thousand black beetles were going to take a long time to find.

16. Two Thousand
Black Beetles

MRS PRICE was quite upset when the children began to search the house for black beetles.

'You won't find those dirty things in our house!' she exclaimed, and demanded what they wanted them for.

Deborah and Jeff were speechless, and looked at Samantha.

'For a Project,' said Samantha promptly. 'For a project for Miss Mellor!'

'The things they teach children nowadays!' Mrs Price said helplessly to Mr Price. 'Now what kind of an education can you get out of nasty dirty old black beetles?'

'Used to see plenty when I was a lad!' said Mr Price, 'but they seem to have died out. Have you noticed how, whenever something seems to die out nice and decent, the whole country starts up a project to get it going again? Black beetles! Let 'em show a leg in my drains and they'll get what's coming to 'em!'

But quite undaunted Samantha told Miss Mellor that the Park was open to the study of bogwoppits, and to help the Project on, it might be necessary to capture and collect a very large quantity of black beetles.

'I always thought they must eat some kind of protein besides aruncus wopitus leaves!' she said to the Prices.

'And cornflakes!' said Timothy.

'Oh *cornflakes*!' said Samantha, dismissing the cornflakes.

'You hear what Samantha says?' Miss Mellor addressed the class. 'Let's see who can bring the largest number of black beetles to school in the morning, shall we? And meanwhile, since Samantha's auntie has given us permission to go into the Park, we will start our Project straight away this afternoon.'

The class cheered. They were all anxious to see the bogwoppit again, and thought Samantha had been very secretive about it.

They set off after dinner with Miss Mellor, a number of notebooks, pencils, and actually four black beetles that somebody had found under the carpentry shop. Samantha took charge of these. She did not want them cast into the marsh pool and wasted. It was most unlikely that the bogwoppits could count. Therefore it was most important to present a large number of black beetles all together.

The marsh pools, as might have been expected, were absolutely deserted. The class spent some time looking for footprints in the mud, but there was nothing that could not have been made by moorhens or coots. Duckweed was settling on the patches of water. Nothing seemed to have disturbed the surface of the pools for a long time. Yet not so long ago the water had been rippled by a bogwoppit claw, or wing, and all the Prices as well as Samantha had seen the pale blue eyes beneath the duckweed, and watched the bottle with its message snatched from view.

The class were confident at first, but then lost faith. They grew tired of sitting around and watching the quiet pools. The camera owner dropped his camera in the wet. Miss Mellor chatted to Samantha and the Prices about the bogwoppit and read aloud the very short account of it in her natural history book.

'It says,' she reminded them, 'that it is believed to be extinct, and as it is four o'clock and time to go home, I'm afraid that extinct it will have to remain for us this afternoon!'

At that moment, quite suddenly, the surface of the water was violently disturbed. A round, black furry head shot out of the middle of a patch of duckweed. Two round blue eyes focused for a moment on the class, and then turned towards Samantha. With a bound and a great splashing of black mud and green duckweed the One-and-Only-Bogwoppit emerged from the pond, shot straight through the middle of Miss Mellor's legs, causing her to sit down very suddenly on the grass, and leapt at Samantha. For a moment its wet black feet and whirring wings clambered up her dress as up a ladder. Then its head was rootling under her chin, seeking her ear, as with piteous and loving cries it plastered her with its dirty feathers and a variety of kisses, known only to bogwoppits and their kind.

Rubbing its beak finally over her cheeks it slid backwards down her dress, ripping it at the hem, and floundered away into the pond. There it sank like a stone without even a backward glance.

'It loves me!' sang Samantha's heart.

The class was utterly dumbfounded.

Miss Mellor was primarily concerned with wiping the mud off Samantha's school dress with her handkerchief, and assuring herself that nobody had been hurt. She could imagine Lady Clandorris suing the school for allowing her niece Samantha to be savagely attacked by a bogwoppit.

But Samantha was not hurt at all. The marks on her face were not bites but dirty kisses, and she was beaming for joy.

'Well there! You all saw it for yourselves!' said Miss Mellor, greatly relieved. 'And we can't stop any longer this afternoon, though it looks exactly like the description that is written in my book. First thing in the morning I am going to ask you all to write a description of what it looked like to *you*. And next time we had better all come in wellies and macintoshes!'

She offered to come up to the Park with Samantha and explain to Lady Clandorris about the state of Samantha's dress, but Samantha said it was quite all right and her aunt would not be at all angry. Deborah Price giggled, and then turned scarlet as everyone looked at her. Miss Mellor pretended not to notice. She was actually extremely excited by the events of the afternoon, and was anxious to get home to write a letter to the secretary of the S.P.R.R.L. (The Society for the Preservation of Rare and Rural Life) of which she was a member. People who were not members called them the Sprawlies.

Because they had actually seen a bogwoppit all the children became enthusiastic about beetle hunting, but in spite of their enthusiasm and massed searching there were only a hundred and seventy-five black beetles brought to Samantha in the school playground the next morning. And a note she had found stuck in the bars of the grid had produced the words: CAN'T YOU HURRY UP. I WANT TO GET OUT. It sounded testy.

Samantha realized that timing was going to play an important part in the rescue. If they handed over the ransom too quickly (and this did not seem in the least probable at present), Aunt Daisy might not be grateful enough, and things would quickly slide back to the way they had been before. If they took too long about it Lady Clandorris might accuse them of doing it on purpose, and keeping her a prisoner for their own ends. In that case she was not at all likely to ask Samantha to come back and live at the Park. The ideal would be to collect the right amount of black beetles within the next few days and then to present their own conditions before handing them over. After all, Lady Clandorris had much more to gain from her freedom than they had.

Samantha wrote another note: VERY DIFFICULT TO COLLECT RANSOM. DOING OUR BEST.

Back came the answer in a matter of minutes.

THE HOUSE IS FULL OF THEM, YOU STUPID CHILD.

Samantha sighed in exasperation. She knew there were vast colonies of black beetles in the Park, but catching them was quite another matter. While she cornered one the rest made off and disappeared at a surprising rate. The same thing happened in every cupboard she opened. She complained bitterly to the Prices, who had not given any help at all, being glued to a television serial that meant a great deal to them at the moment.

'I think we ought to tell my dad!' said Timothy when she reproached them.

'Not yet!' said Samantha hastily, 'I've got a better idea first. We'll have a beetle drive!'

'Where?'

'At the Park!'

'When?'

'After school tomorrow!'

When she put the suggestion before them the class was not so enthusiastic as they had been the first time Samantha had invited them to her home. It was partly, perhaps, because she had mentioned that this time there would be no tea, and partly because Lady Clandorris's sudden appearance and the subsequent disgracing of Samantha had left rather an unpleasant memory. But she assured them that this time Lady Clandorris had gone right away, and that she now went in and out as she pleased.

But since they had explored it for themselves the Park was no longer the place of glamour and mystery they had imagined it to be. They remembered, not so much the lofty rooms, the halls, the staircase and even the pianola, but also the dust, the dereliction and the squalor, as well as the wrath and indignation of Lady Clandorris in the face of all her uninvited visitors.

'Come on! It will be fun!' Samantha coaxed them. 'Besides, when we've collected the black beetles we can get the bogwoppits to come to the surface any time we want them. We can *tame* them!'

But the class remembered the rather violent appearance of the One-and-Only-Bogwoppit, and did not seem eager to have tame bogwoppits climbing all over them. Their mothers, they decided, would detest it. Miss Mellor had mentioned something about building a hide and watching the bogwoppits through slits in the walls. This, the class decided, was a much more sensible way of carrying out the Project.

'All right,' Samantha said suddenly. 'There will be food after all.'

The class gave in. They agreed to go up to the Park the next day, after school, carrying polythene bags in which to capture the black beetles.

Samantha was triumphant. Once more she warned the Prices to keep the subject of Lady Clandorris's kidnapping a secret. She told the whole class to arrive at the Park by four o'clock the next day. The twins' class was included at the last minute, for fear that Tim would tell his father, out of revenge. The mere thought of another feast and of playing the pianola was enough to win everybody's approval and acceptance.

It was left to Samantha to think out the question of food and drink. She had no idea where this was to come from. Kind Mrs Price might supply a few cakes or biscuits, but not supplies for a party of nearly sixty children.

Fortunately, on her return to the Prices' home she met Mr Beaumont, Lady Clandorris's lawyer, on the doorstep. He had been handing

Mrs Price the monthly cheque for Samantha's keep.

'Ah, young lady!' he said on seeing Samantha. 'We had just been talking over the question of your pocket money! How is your auntie?'

Samantha immediately sensed that Mr Beaumont did not want to go up to the Park and find out for himself.

'My auntie is all right,' said Samantha. 'What about my pocket money?'

Mrs Price tactfully withdrew. Mr Beaumont and Samantha walked in the garden.

'Do you find it enough?' asked Mr Beaumont. 'Your auntie told me to give you what the other children have, and any more that may be necessary.'

'Necessary for what?' asked Samantha cautiously.

'Well, perhaps you want to go for a bus ride now and then?' Mr Beaumont suggested. 'Or get some clothes? Or go to the pictures?'

'Yes I do!' said Samantha. 'I want to get a new dress and to take all the Prices to the pictures.'

'Well that's rather a tall order!' said Mr Beaumont, looking alarmed.

'All right, I can do without the dress!' said Samantha. 'But I'd like to take them all out to tea after the pictures.'

'All of them? Mum, Dad and the children?' said Mr Beaumont.

'All of them,' said Samantha subbornly.

'Of course, they have been very good to you!' agreed Mr Beaumont thoughtfully. 'Very good indeed.' Privately he was sorry for Samantha. He thought she had been poorly treated by her aunt, and was not averse to spending some of Lady Clandorris's money on her if necessary. 'You can spend what you like to get the child looked after,' Lady Clandorris had told him. 'Just as long as I don't set eyes on her again.'

Between them Mr Beaumont and Samantha worked out how much money it would take to buy cinema tickets for the five Prices and herself and to take them out to tea afterwards. Samantha reminded him that there would also be bus fares.

'It *is* a lot of money!' Mr Beaumont sighed at the end of their calculations.

'Not for six people and tea as well as the cinema and the bus both ways,' said Samantha. 'I shan't do it every week.'

'I should think not!' said Mr Beaumont, but he handed over the money without further argument.

'You will have to wait a little longer for your new dress!' he told her, adding with a fatherly smile: 'We'll let Auntie get over this one first!'

Samantha raced Mr Beaumont to the gate in her hurry to get down to the shops and lay out the money in cakes, biscuits, potato crisps and bottles of fizzy lemonade. She was too accustomed to running rings round Aunt Lily to worry about buying them under false pretences. She was glad to find that there was just enough money left over to take Mrs Price, by herself, to the pictures at a later date.

She hurried up to the Park, carrying trays, and closely followed by the Prices.

The beetle drive was a great success. Samantha announced that anyone catching ten beetles was eligible to play a whole roll of music on the pianola. Presently there was a whole queue of people awaiting their turn, and Samantha went into the kitchen to find a larger container for all the black beetles they had collected. The kitchen was pervaded by a familiar smell, and beyond the cellar door a familiar moaning and wailing filled her with apprehension.

Sure enough, when she opened the door, the thinnest, flattest bogwoppit she had ever seen sat whimpering in a puddle on the far side. It had evidently squeezed through the bars of the grid, and was holding a piece of paper in its beak.

Samantha snatched the paper and closed the cellar door on the bogwoppit, but it set up such a caterwauling that she was forced to open it again. As she did so Timothy entered the kitchen behind her, bent upon refreshments.

'It squeezed through the grid,' Samantha said, half in and half out of the cellar door. 'I don't know how . . . but it has!'

'We ought to tell my dad!' said Timothy.

'Read this first!' said Samantha, holding out the paper.

The words on it said:

I WANT MY HAT FOR EMERGING.

'What does "emerging" mean?' asked Timothy.

'Getting out, you twit. Go upstairs and get the hat with feathers on it. It's on her bed. I'll look after the bogwoppit,' said Samantha. 'Don't let anyone see you with the hat!' she hissed after him as he made for the stairs.

Tim came back with the pheasant feather hat crushed under his blazer. Nobody had seen him come or go. Samantha took it from him and spruced it up with the hearth brush. It was a very old and dusty hat like everything else belonging to Lady Clandorris. Some of the pheasants' feathers were coming out.

'It will be ruined if the bogwoppit drags it through the bars!' Samantha said. 'I'd better go and unlock the grid for it.'

'What about tea?' said Timothy.

'When I come back!' said Samantha, keeping a fast hold on the hat, and following the bogwoppit through the cellar door. She kept the key of the grid high on the dresser, and was now carrying it in the left-hand pocket of her jeans.

Arriving at the grid the long, thin bogwoppit insisted on wriggling through the bars, just to show her how clever it was, but Samantha firmly refused to push the hat after it. She unlocked the gate in the grid and passed through it Lady Clandorris's pheasant feather hat.

By the beam of her torch she saw the bogwoppit put the hat saucily on its head and prance away down the tunnel.

But it was hardly out of sight before she heard a banshee screech of rage, followed by one of terror. Yelp followed snarl, scuffling broke out and the drain reverberated to the sound of fighting. Triumphant cries mingled with vanquished sobbing, and then the noise died down.

Full of misgivings, Samantha was in half a mind to penetrate the drain a little farther beyond the grid, but she was afraid the bogwoppits might rush at her in the dark and take the key away, or, worse still, overpower her and make her a prisoner like Lady Clandorris. So she locked the gate very firmly and was turning away, when a scampering noise arrested her. Something came galloping up the drain in the darkness to hurl itself with full force against the bars of the grid.

Samantha's torch shone full into the round blue eyes and beaky bill of the One-and-Only, not loving and affectionate now, but crumpled and indignant, as with bill and wing and angry claw it thrust the unfortunate remains of Lady Clandorris's pheasant feather hat through the bars in several dozen pieces.

'Oh how *naughty* you are!' Samantha scolded, but the One-and-Only did not wait to be reproved. It flounced away into the darkness in a series of scornful leaps and bounces, leaving Samantha to pick up such fragments as she could find by the feeble light of her torch, and to find her way back to the kitchen, where her guests were beginning to assemble and clamour for their tea.

The result of the beetle drive was just under two thousand black beetles of every shape and size. Some of them were alive and some were dead. The ransom had not stipulated anything about condition.

17. Fame at Last!

SUDDENLY the park became the centre of a great deal of interest, from a great many different sources.

Miss Mellor reported her Project to the Society for the Protection of Rare and Rural Species, who told her at once that bogwoppits were extinct, and that even if they were not, they were a protected animal and nobody was allowed to kill them.

This was a great relief to Samantha, but she was very much afraid that it would not prevent her aunt from sluicing the cellar out with disinfectant just whenever she felt like it, once she was free and in her own territory again.

There had been no message since the hat incident, and everything seemed quiet down the drain. Samantha kept the two thousand black beetles in a box in her bedroom, and pondered on the best moment to offer up the ransom.

Overnight, it seemed, the Park became crowded with people. It was all coming true, just as Samantha had dreamed it; first the Preservation Society in a van, then a television company. They put up tents and hides in the Park all round the marsh pools, and kept coming up to the house to ask Lady Clandorris's permission for being there at all.

Slowly it was appreciated that Lady Clandorris was not in residence, and had not been there, in fact, for a long time. Bills were unpaid, letters from months back lay in the letter box, and all rateable amenities had been cut off by the appropriate authorities.

Samantha was asked all kinds of questions, but pretended to know nothing at all about her aunt. She agreed that she had been up at the Park, but thought her aunt had gone away on a visit. No, she didn't know when she would be back again. She explained that she herself was staying with the Prices, and just went up now and again to have a look round the place.

When the Preservation Society heard that it was Samantha who had discovered the bogwoppits they took her photograph, which appeared in the national press, and it looked very much as if she and the Prices, as well as Miss Mellor, might all appear on television.

Samantha and the Prices said nothing about the cellar or the grid, or Lady Clandorris being kept as a prisoner down there somewhere underneath their feet. Even Timothy realized that once the truth came out there would soon be an end to the tents in the Park and the television appearance and all the fame and the fun. It would very likely be the end of the bogwoppits as well.

But Samantha's usually robust conscience was for once uneasy, and she began to plan the right moment for offering her black beetles and driving a bargain at the same time with her aunt that would keep everybody satisfied, if not exactly happy.

When Mrs Price realized that Lady Clandorris was no longer at the Park she was quite upset, and refused to let Samantha sleep up there alone. Samantha missed living in the house and playing at being lady-of-the-manor to all the new arrivals, but she went up every evening after tea. Sometimes she went down the drain and looked for the One-and-Only, and one unforgettable evening she actually saw it and was able to kiss it through the bars, but it was not safe to let it out with so many strangers about.

The other bogwoppits were becoming much more friendly. They began to come to the grid and make cheerful little noises as if they were glad to see her. Sometimes she fed them with black beetles, to sharpen their appreciation. But of her aunt she neither heard nor saw a sign.

Once she wrote a note and sent it by the One-and-Only.

DEAR AUNT DAISY. ARE YOU STILL ALL RIGHT?

Nothing happened. But two days later an empty cereal carton floated on the surface of the marsh pool. Written across it was the one word: YES. It did not mean anything to anybody except Samantha.

Meanwhile, the Society for the Preservation of Rare and Rural Species and the television people were kept excited and happy by occasional glimpses of bogwoppits in the pools, usually just underneath the surface, and usually when the sun went down. Once they were filmed actually eating aruncus wopitus, much to the envy of Miss Mellor, who still had only the muddy flurry of a bogwoppit diving under the water recorded on her instamatic camera.

The time was drawing near, Samantha reluctantly admitted to herself, when she must make a definite move. She hoped to be able to turn it to her own advantage, but meanwhile she sent a further message down the drain: RANSOM READY. WHAT NOW?

Nothing happened. She tried again, less tersely: DEAR AUNT DAISY. THE RANSOM IS READY. WHEN WOULD YOU LIKE TO BE RESCUED?

'When she says when,' Samantha told the Prices, 'I shall tell her my terms. She has got to let me live with her again. I like living with you and I love your mum, but the Park is my home.'

The Prices agreed that this was true, but they were really thinking about the pianola.

To their astonishment a note came back by way of the grid. Written on it in firm black letters were two words only:

TOO LATE.

Samantha stared and stared, so did the Prices. What could it possibly mean?

'Do you think she can be dead?' asked Deborah.

'It's her writing! She wrote it!' said Samantha sturdily. 'There's something else up and we'll have to find out what it is.'

A further proof of Aunt Daisy's aliveness were the number of cans and empty cereal packets floating about on the surface of the marsh pools, with which the bogwoppits played a kind of water polo, to the great delight of the television and film company. The Preservation Society accused them of leaving their litter about, and were very caustic about vandalism.

Samantha wrote another letter, putting it into the now friendly beak of a bogwoppit at

the grid. WHAT SHALL WE DO NOW?
she wrote.

The reply was even more surprising than
the last:

YOU CAN LEAVE ME ALONE AND
GO AWAY.

Samantha and the Prices simply did not
know what to make of it. That night it began
to rain.

It must have been very disagreeable
for the people camping in the Park. For a
while they braved the weather, taking
endless films of the bogwoppits splashing and
sporting in the marsh pools, enjoying their
favourite weather, but first Miss Mellor and
then the rest of the Preservation Society
abandoned their projects, and sat it out in
their tents waiting for finer weather. The
film people took what pictures they could
in the rain, but there was a limit to shots
of bubbling mud and wallowing bogwoppits,
whose antics became a little monotonous.

They too retired to their tents, while the rain went on and on and on.

Samantha, just a little worried by the turn things had taken, slopped up to the Park in gumboots, keeping an eye on the cellar, but no bogwoppits came to the grid, and a message she sent to her aunt asking after her health remained uncollected between the bars. Then it really became too wet to go up to the Park at all, so she stayed away.

It rained for nearly a week. On the seventh day she found a little piece of paper floating on the marsh pools. It might have been there for days. The word on it was nearly washed out. It just said: HELP!

Samantha's heart stood still. Her first thought was to run straight up to the Park, and her next was to find Jeff Price and ask him to go with her. But the film company were showing the films they had taken, in the village hall, and Samantha had been on her way to join them when she had digressed by way of the marsh pools, hoping, but hardly expecting, to catch a glimpse of the One-and-Only, who had been invisible for so long that she was very much afraid it had forgotten all about her.

When she looked in at the village hall door, Jeff Price was sitting in the front row with his mouth open, staring at the screen. In fact everybody was sitting there perfectly absorbed, and nobody noticed Samantha peep in and then turn round and run away.

She did not wait to fetch her gumboots, but splashed up the muddy drive, soaking herself to her knees, and never stopped until she reached the door of the house. She pushed it open, ran across the hall into the kitchen, and down the cellar steps.

And here her worst fears were realized. Bitterly now she blamed herself for neglecting to pay her previous daily visits to the Park. The heavy rain had swollen the stream and the gulleys and the culverts. It had flooded the passage, and the cellar was inches deep in water.

Samantha seized the torch, more feeble now as the battery was wearing out. She wrenched open the door to the long tunnel, up which the water flowed in a sinister flood. Regretting her gumboots she braved the darkness, feeling the cold lapping of the water creeping up her ankles like icy fingers. The way was familiar or she would have been too frightened for such a venture, but she felt she knew every inch as far as the grid, so battled gallantly on, till the light from the cellar stairs had long since faded out behind her, and at long long last the beam of her torch shone on the bars of Mr Price's gate.

It was at this moment that she realized that she no longer had the key in her pocket. Where and when she had lost it she did not know but it certainly was not with her now.

In the moment of shock everything seemed to stand still, even the water lapping at her feet. And then Samantha seized the bars in both hands, dropping the torch in her agony, so that it sank beneath the water and gleamed up at her like the watchful eyes of bogwoppits. Samantha shook and shook the bars, but Mr Price's grid stood firm.

'Aunt Daisy!' shouted Samantha. The cry rang along the wet, dark drain ahead, as if miles beyond the bend it was passed along from echo to echo.

'Aunt Daisy!' she called again, and yet again. The echo carried her cry farther and farther into the darkness, and from far, far away in the remoteness beyond came back an answer.

Samantha had to strain her ears to hear it, and even then she hardly believed the words that she heard. But they were repeated again and again, and there was such a note of pleading and despair in the voice that she seized the bars and shook them until she was dizzy with the effort.

'SAMANTHA! OH, DO PLEASE COME, SAMANTHA!'

And before the voice died away a new sound joined the sad duet, a sound of water flopping, flapping, coming nearer and nearer. The next moment a familiar black wing was thrust through the grid.

Samantha had rescued her torch, and the feeble beam was reflected in the round blue eyes of the One-and-Only, its rubbery beak offering frantic kisses through the bars, its wet, webbed feet trying to reach and embrace her.

It was such a long time since she had seen it that Samantha's frantic anxiety turned to joy. She fondled and kissed such damp feathers as she could reach, trying to explain that she was unable to get through the gate and take it into her arms. The bogwoppit grew excited and seemed to be getting impatient with her. When at last it realized that all its efforts were useless, and Samantha was not going to open the gate and cuddle it, it splashed away, giving her one long, last reproachful look over its shoulder. And once again out of the darkness came the cry:

SAMANTHA! OH, SAMANTHA, DO COME!

The key! Oh, the key! In vain Samantha searched her pockets. There was no key, and she could not even remember the last time she had handled it. Perhaps there was a file in the kitchen at the Park and she could saw through the bars? But filing was a man's job rather than a girl's. If only she had made Jeff come with her – two pairs of hands were better than one. He would have known, for instance, what his father did to open iron bars when a key was lost. And thinking of Mr Price reminded Samantha that of course there was another key! Mr Price had one too, and she must find him and get it from him just as quickly as she possibly could.

It was the half-term holiday week. All the children were free, but of course Mr Price was working just as usual. Mrs Price, less calm than was her habit due to washing and the wet weather, was thankful for the village hall film show which kept the four wet children from getting under her feet all the morning. She was anything but pleased to see Samantha come flying into the house quite plastered with mud, and apparently soaked to the skin from the ankles upwards.

'The keys!' she panted. 'Where does Mr Price keep his keys?'

Mrs Price stared at her, dustpan and brush in hand. 'The *keys*!' repeated Samantha, speaking more vigorously than she had ever spoken to Mrs Price before.

When children shouted at her, Mrs Price did not shout back like Aunt Lily did. She merely became remote and distant. This time she went on brushing the hearthrug and said nothing at all to Samantha.

'Where are the *keys*?' wailed Samantha, with such agony in her voice that Mrs Price took notice of her at last.

'What keys?' she asked stiffly.

'The keys of the cellar! Mr Price's keys!' wailed Samantha.

'Mr Price's keys are with Mr Price, where they belong!' said Mrs Price, brushing smartly.

'Where's Mr Price? Oh do please tell me where he is!' pleaded Samantha. Mrs Price had never seen her so excitable and upset. She stopped brushing the hearthrug.

'Now don't get yourself into such a state!' she said in some surprise. 'You can't go running off after him in all this rain. He's gone over to the vicarage at Chopley, and he won't be back till teatime. You go and change yourself out of those wet clothes, Sammy, and we'll have a cup of tea.'

But Samantha's agitation became even greater.

'Please will you lend me your bicycle, Mrs Price? Oh please do,' she urged, almost clasping Mrs Price in her arms as she pleaded.

'You don't want to bicycle all that way with the rain coming down like this!' said Mrs Price in astonishment, but as she did not directly refuse, Samantha took her hesitation as permission, and charged out of the house, snatched Mrs Price's bicycle from the shed, and pedalled away furiously on the five mile ride to Chopley.

The rain poured down her face, her neck and shoulders and down her back. It splashed off the road until her legs were just as wet as if she had still been paddling down the drain. Every car that passed her deluged her with water, while a finer spray from oncoming vehicles was just as disagreeable and unpleasant.

In Chopley she had to ask her way twice to the vicarage, only to find that Mr Price had broken off work for the lunch hour and had taken his sandwiches off to eat at the Green Dragon.

He was washing them down with a pint of beer in company with some mates when the door opened and in came Samantha. She was dripping from head to foot and spattered all over with mud.

'Mr Price! I want the key of the drain!' she said without preamble.

Mr Price stared at her, a bite taken out of his second sandwich and suspended as it were in mid air.

'What drain?' he asked, to gain time. He was so completely flabbergasted by the sight of Samantha.

'You aren't allowed in here, you know!' the barman told Samantha quite severely. 'Children aren't allowed in the public bar!'

Mr Price followed Samantha outside. She was so obviously distressed, but he could not fathom what it was she really wanted.

She pulled herself together and tried to speak to him coherently.

'Please will you give me the key to the grid you made in my aunt, Lady Clandorris's, cellar, in the Park?' she said. 'The one that unlocks the gate in the great drain? I've lost mine and I've simply got to open the drain as quickly as possible!'

'And what have you got to open my grid for, young Samantha?' said Mr Price, slowly and suspiciously. 'That gate wasn't made to be opened, only for repairs, and *you* never had a key that I know of. I gave one to her Ladyship, not to you. I can't see any reason for you having a key to open the gate in my grid. There isn't any call for it!'

'But there is! There is!' cried Samantha in desperation. 'My Aunt Daisy is down there at the bottom of the drain, and the bogwoppits are holding her for ransom!'

18. The Rescuing of Lady Clandorris

I N THE end Mr Price gave the key to Samantha to quieten her, she was getting so hysterical. Privately he had always thought her a little mad, though he liked her well enough.

She could not persuade him to leave his job and help her. Her excitement was so intense that he simply did not believe her story. He couldn't leave the vicarage sink half done, he said stubbornly, and even her tears did not

wholly move him. Whatever was wrong up at
the Park he would come and have a look at it
in the evening, and this was the best that she
could get out of him. Thankful that at least
she had possession of the key, she pedalled
homewards as fast as she could go.

'You take young Jeff with you if you are
going down that mucky cellar!' Mr Price
called after her, taking his last sandwich back
into the pub.

'Oh I will! I will!' cried Samantha, but by
the time she had pedalled back to the Park
with the wind in her face she did not feel
inclined to ride another half mile to the village
in search of Jeff. She had been such a long
time away, and the cry for help had been so
despairing.

Propping Mrs Price's bicycle against the
front door steps she entered the house and
squelched noisily down the steps towards the
rising water in the cellar.

Before she went into the drain she discovered and lit a small paraffin hand lamp, so she put the torch into her pocket as a second string, and paddled into the tunnel, trying not to splash too much for fear the glass chimney should crack.

The water was deeper now, and felt very cold. It took much longer to wade along the flooded passage than to walk down it on dry feet. The flood seemed to drag at her ankles and nibble at the calves of her legs. It swirled at her as if telling her to go home.

Presently she came to the grid. Everything was quiet now, but she began to realize that once the gate was open she would be at the mercy, not only of the flood, but of the bogwoppits. Would they be gentle and friendly as they had been of late, or rough and boisterous as on the Day of the Hat? She wished she had brought the bag of black beetles from her bedroom in Mrs Price's house. And she wished she had taken Mr Price's advice and gone to fetch Jeff first.

Who would ever find out if something happened to her down here in this dreadful place? Would Aunt Daisy know? And would she care if she did?

Samantha listened. No sound at all. Had the noise of her splashing made no echo?

Before putting the key in the lock she called again, gently at first and then much louder:

'Aunt Daisy! Are you there?'

Far, far away came the piteous reply:

'SAMANTHA! OH, SAMANTHA! HELP!'

It was enough. With her left hand Samantha put the key in the lock and turned it, holding the lamp aloft in her right. Then carefully opening the barred gate in the grid, she bent her head and scrambled through the entrance. This time she kept the key tightly clasped in her hand until she had deposited it safely inside her pocket. The water came swirling towards her. Samantha splashed through it, round one bend after another, till she came to a fork in the drain. The left-hand tunnel seemed to flow slightly uphill, with the water pumping and gurgling round her legs, but some of it flowed back into the right-hand fork, over a broken and jagged step, as if somewhere, once, there had been a retaining wall, but far ahead along this passage Samantha could see a reflection on the distant walls, as if some way beyond her, round some bend or another, there was a light.

Towards this light Samantha advanced, the water growing deeper and deeper round her calves as the passage appeared to slope downhill and then suddenly she turned a corner and was in a large round chamber whose only illumination was a small brass handlamp like her own, perched on the top of a pile of boxes that she immediately recognized as stores from Lady Clandorris's cupboards at the Park. The whole room was lined with boxes, against which the flood water lapped greedily, as if licking its lips at the sight of the labels and their contents.

In the very middle of the room, on a pile of boxes shaped very much like a throne, dressed in her dressing gown, with a feather boa round her shoulders and several jumpers and dresses underneath, sat her Aunt Daisy, Lady Clandorris, with her toes drawn up tightly to avoid the water, and the One-and-Only-Bogwoppit curled up fast asleep in her lap.

'Aunt Daisy!' said Samantha faintly. Her throat felt suddenly tight and constricted as if she were going to cry, and she had a surprising urge to rush forward and put her arms around Lady Clandorris's neck. She had hardly taken in the fact that there were no other bogwoppits to be seen.

'Aunt Daisy!' she said again in a quavering voice. 'I've come to rescue you!'

'Well you might have come sooner!' snapped Lady Clandorris. 'All my pillows are wet! The water is still rising! I want you to go and tell that plumber man to come straight up here and cement up the wall between here and the main drain so the water can't get in.'

'But then you can't get out!' said Samantha in amazement.

'Out! I don't want to get out!' said Lady Clandorris. 'And nobody can get in either. All those other little monsters can stay out too. They think of nothing these days but having their photographs taken and fooling about in the marsh pools.'

'Do you *know* about the photographers?' asked Samantha, astonished.

'Well what do you think?' said Lady Clandorris. 'One can't live in the company of bogwoppits day in, day out all these weeks without learning something of their language. Besides, Boggy tells me everything, don't you, Boggy?'

The One-and-Only woke up and gave a tremendous yawn. It stretched out a foot and shrieked as its toe touched the water. One would have thought it had never met cold water in the whole of its life before.

Then it saw Samantha, gave an outsize leap that nearly dashed the handlamp from her hand, landed on her shoulder, embraced her, licked her face all over, rubbed its beak and wet feathers all over her neck and chin, and returned like a feathered torpedo to Lady Clandorris's lap.

'It seems to like you!' said Lady Clandorris with some displeasure. 'I can't think why!' Samantha was silent.

'Well – say something!' said her aunt impatiently. 'I suppose you are hungry and want some dinner. I've had mine. You will have to help yourself. The can opener is down there somewhere in the water.'

'You called me!' said Samantha accusingly.

'Yes, of course I did! I was afraid of being drowned,' said Lady Clandorris. 'And I wanted you to fetch the plumber.'

'I've come to rescue you!' said Samantha. All the conditions of rescue she had been going to present seeped away. There was something about her Aunt Daisy that precluded bargaining. 'If you come now you'll be all right,' she said. 'I've unlocked the gate.'

'Then lock it up again, you stupid child!' shrieked Lady Clandorris. 'All those little nasties will be swimming up into the Park! I want the plumber to build up the wall just as it used to be, and then they'll have to stay in the marsh pools and Boggy and I will be all dry and comfortable in here. Won't we, Boggy?'

The One-and-Only twisted on to its back like a cat and stretched its wings. Samantha felt a sharp stab of jealousy.

'You don't really want to stay here, Aunt Daisy?' she asked incredulously.

'Why not? I like it. I didn't at first when those little pests captured me and were so rough and wild. But they're different now.

They are fond of me, only there are far too many of them. And Boggy loves me, don't you, Boggy?'

The One-and-Only burrowed its beak into her neck. Then it turned towards Samantha and blinked its pale blue eyes fondly at her. She thought it was trying to say: 'I love you too!'

'Nobody loves me up there!' said Lady Clandorris, suddenly plaintive. 'Only my sister Gertie and she never did anything for me and gave all our mother's jewellery to Lily, when I ought to have had it, being the eldest. Your Uncle Ernest, he didn't love me either, he went off to South America all by himself and left me in that dreary old Park.'

'I love the Park!' said Samantha.

'You can have it!' said Lady Clandorris. 'I'll make it over to you lock, stock and barrel, and you needn't worry – I shan't ask for it back. I've had enough of being asked to have garden fêtes and Boy Scout camps and Rolls

Royce rallies and all that paraphernalia in my private home and garden. No peace anywhere, except down here. I like it.'

'I can't live up in the Park while you are living down here in the drain!' said Samantha, appalled at the prospect.

'Why not? You can ask your Mr and Mrs Price to come and caretake the place and open it to the National Trust on Sundays. You can rent out the grounds to all those film people and the campers and the Preservation Trusts, and that will pay for the upkeep. You can charge them to come and look at the bogwoppits. Make it a safari park, or a bogwoppitry, call it anything you like as long as I don't have to look at it. Forget me!'

'I can't forget you!' said Samantha slowly.

The glass shade of the lamp in her hand was blackening in the smoke of the flame, and she could see it was because her hand was trembling.

'Why not?' snapped Lady Clandorris.

'I don't know!' said Samantha. 'But if I could have forgotten you I would not have come all this way to rescue you, would I?'

There was a long silence.

'I think you are drowning!' said Samantha.

'Nobody would care if I did!' said Lady Clandorris bitterly.

'You can't expect them to care, can you? Why should they?' cried Samantha. 'You've never done anything nice for anyone else; why should they come and rescue you? You've always been horrible to me!' she shouted over her shoulder, beginning to wade back into the tunnel. 'I wanted to be your long-lost niece and make life more enjoyable for you. After all, I am your sister Gertie's child!' she yelled as she retreated, stumbling in the water and nearly losing her lamp. 'But you didn't want me and I don't want you either! You can stay with the bogwoppit and drown! The bogwoppit can swim but I don't know if you can! Goodbye! I'm going home!'

'Fetch the plumber!' shouted Lady Clandorris angrily.

'He's over at Chopley. I cycled all the way over there in the rain to tell him, but he won't come till he's finished the vicarage sink. That won't be till teatime!' called Samantha at the top of her voice, retreating all the time in the direction of the tunnel. 'I'm going home anyway,' she repeated.

There was an agonized cry as the One-and-Only leapt from Lady Clandorris's lap on to Samantha's shoulders, nearly choking her with its flapping wings, and almost putting out the lamp. Then with a splash it swam the short distance back to Lady Clandorris, before once again chasing Samantha with cries of distress. At last it seized Lady Clandorris by the sodden hem of her dressing gown and tried to drag her into the water after Samantha.

'I'm only coming as far as the kitchen, to dry my stockings while you fetch the plumber!' Aunt Daisy said, splashing through the flood, but Samantha was well ahead and out of hearing.

Far up the second fork of the drain she had heard the ominous murmur of voices she knew too well. The bogwoppits were returning from the marsh pools, and she put all the effort she could muster into reaching the grid before they came.

Lady Clandorris seemed to realize the threat and its consequences.

Suddenly she ceased to scold and grumble, but hurried after Samantha looking fearfully backwards across her shoulder as she came to the fork in the drain. The One-and-Only was urging her on with little whimpering cries, swimming between her and Samantha, who was forced to slow down, quite against her will, rather than abandon her, once she knew her aunt was really coming. She began to be really frightened. The noises behind her were getting louder. The bogwoppits were returning to their home, but as yet they had no idea that their prisoner was escaping.

'Can't you hurry, Aunt Daisy?' she urged her in the echoing passage.

'It wouldn't have been necessary to hurry if you had done as I asked and fetched the plumber!' grumbled Lady Clandorris, but she too looked uneasily backwards into the solid darkness, and splashed on a little more noisily than before.

The One-and-Only was mewing with anxiety. Samantha tried to catch it, but she only had one free hand, and it slipped out of her grasp, swimming back towards Aunt Daisy and frantically tugging at her clothes.

Suddenly Lady Clandorris tripped and pitched over, falling on her face in the water. It took the combined powers of Samantha and the bogwoppit to set her on her feet again.

A curve in the drain muffled the squeaking and babbling behind them, or perhaps the bogwoppits had arrived at the fork and turned back into the great chamber in which they had left their prisoner.

Sure enough, indignant screams and protests rose suddenly from the shadows behind them. The next moment a sound like a pack of hounds in full cry reverberated down the drain, echoed by the splashing and the plashing of a hundred swimming furry bodies.

19. Out of the Drain

LADY Clandorris stumbled again in sudden fear. The noise was so appalling and so close behind them. To rescue her from the water Samantha was forced to use both hands, or her aunt would have sunk underneath the flood. The lamp went out with a hiss as it touched the water, and the chimney cracked with the snap of a bullet.

Now they were in pitch darkness, but the only way was forwards with the stream. Fortunately the sides of the passage gave them a guide and they could only stumble on and on. Samantha supported her aunt, dragging her along and encouraging her. She surprised herself by all the brave and courageous things she found to say.

'We are nearly at the grid!' she told Aunt Daisy a dozen times. 'We only have to lock the gate behind us to keep them out! I have the key safe in my pocket! Come on – hurry! Hurry! Oh *hurry*! You're doing fine!' The bogwoppit swam close behind them, whimpering under its breath. It sounded very frightened.

'They'll kill Boggy for letting me out!' Lady Clandorris snuffled. 'They never really trusted him because he was fond of *you*. They knew you were trying to rescue me. I must say, you did take a lot of trouble, Samantha!'

It was the first time she had ever had a word of praise from her aunt, but there was no time to be lost in talking. The grid could not be far away, but how could they tell in the inky blackness? On the other hand the bogwoppits were coming closer and closer, while the One-and-Only's whimpers had turned into shrieks of fear. It pressed closer and closer to Samantha's legs, clawing at her sodden jeans and finally jumping on to her shoulders. The joint burden of carrying the bogwoppit and at the same time supporting her Aunt Daisy was almost more than Samantha could manage alone.

All in a minute the bogwoppits were around her, in a swirling snatching heap, their wet furry bodies encircling her, diving between her legs, leaping over her shoulders. There was nothing she could do but keep a firm clasp of Lady Clandorris and struggle on as best she could, with the One-and-Only half choking her and shrieking blue murder. Suddenly they stumbled against the grid with such an impact that the One-and-Only was thrown against the bars, knocking its head and setting up a howl of pain.

With her own face battered and bruised by a dozen resentful bogwoppits Samantha let go of her aunt to snatch the key from her wet pocket and fumble for the lock. It seemed a long time before she felt the keyhole under her fingers, but it was there, and the key fitted.

Putting her shoulder firmly against the bars, Samantha opened the gate a chink and lowered her head. Then she pushed the cringing One-and-Only through the grid to the far side.

'Now you! ... Quickly!' she told Lady Clandorris, pushing her after it.

Her Aunt Daisy had suddenly come to life and was fighting a rearguard action with the swimming bogwoppits who were trying to drag her backwards along the drain. She showed very much the kind of spirit she must have contributed when she was fighting for her freedom when she was kidnapped. Shouting and scolding she banged their heads together, resisted the flailing of their wings and claws, and seemed actually to be enjoying the battle.

'GO ON!' shouted Samantha, holding open the gate, and trying to push her aunt towards the bars while at the same time preventing the bogwoppits from getting through.

Finally Aunt Daisy fell through backwards, leaving Samantha struggling in the darkness against the army of bogwoppits who were trying in vain to get past her and up the passage to the kitchen.

How long she resisted and struggled she never knew, but suddenly it was over, and she was down in the stream with her head only just above water and a bogwoppit sitting on her chest, while half a dozen more dragged her rapidly backwards through the water along the drain towards the great chamber and the marsh pools.

Samantha heard their triumphant cries, and then came a clang! from the direction of the grid, with more splashing and a furious shouting as the One-and-Only and Lady Clandorris came to her rescue. She was almost dragged in pieces between them all as they joined in the battle, and the struggle in the darkness began all over again.

But above all the shouting and the clamour a strange, new element came stealing down the drain, growing stronger and stronger. It was the smell of disinfectant.

Dropping their prisoner like a hot potato the bogwoppits swam for their lives; in half a minute they were gone, and even the surge of their flight was out of hearing.

Samantha struggled to her feet in time to pick up the One-and-Only and hold it high above the water. It was already gasping for breath as the smell grew stronger.

It flopped panting into her arms, its wings extended, its claws hanging useless. There was nothing Samantha could do but cradle it and murmur helpful promises and endearments while, free at last, she followed her aunt back through the grid, towards the unknown source of their rescue. When a distant beam of a torch could be seen reflected in the water ahead, Samantha fully expected to see Mr Price at the end of it, but instead, a perfectly strange and unknown voice echoed down the drain and the voice said:

'And what the hell is going on down there?'

Lady Clandorris, ablaze with fury and indignation at the conduct of the bogwoppits, was holding the remnants of her dressing gown round the shreds of all her other garments, put on like layers in a sandwich. She was also muttering: 'Savages! Scallywags! Hooligans! Vandals! Dirty, delinquent, devilish little beasts!' But at the sound of the voice she stopped short in her tracks so suddenly that Samantha and the bogwoppit bumped their noses into her back.

'Sorry!' said Samantha automatically.

The bogwoppit gave a feeble moan.

'That,' said Lady Clandorris with the utmost conviction, 'that is the voice of your Uncle Ernest!'

The beam of a powerful torch blinded them as the holder came nearer. When he focused it on the water immediately in front of them Samantha saw, first a large pair of safari boots, then the rising curves of a fairly big stomach, covered in a tweed suit, and finally a round face, pinkish red, even in the shadows, topped by a deerstalker's hat. Behind him, carrying another torch, but rather shrouded by Uncle Ernest's large figure, was, sure enough, the welcome shape of Mr Price.

'What are you doing down here in your dressing gown, Daisy?' Uncle Ernest demanded, standing aside so that Lady Clandorris and Samantha could pass in front of him on their way back to the cellar. 'And who is this wet person with the cat?'

'This is your niece Samantha, Ernest,' said Lady Clandorris. 'My sister Gertie's child. She cares about me. And it is not a cat.'

'It's one of them perishing rats out of the drain the Press are making such a fuss about!'

said Mr Price. He was dumbfounded to find that Samantha had been speaking the truth after all.

When she had left him after telling her garbled tale, he found he could not work, nor even finish his sandwich, suspecting that something was going on up at the Park that concerned his beloved drains. He left the plumbing at the vicarage and went home on his moped, only to find that nobody had seen Samantha since dinner time, in spite of a party given to the children by the film people in the afternoon that might have been particularly likely to attract her.

So Mr Price chugged up the drive in the rain to the Park, arriving at the same moment as a large Range Rover which was drawing up at the steps. Sir Ernest Clandorris was busy getting out of it.

Sir Ernest did not waste too much time in deploring the state of disrepair into which his house had sunk during his absence. Doors were wide open, and the footprints of at least one person were crossing the hall, traversing the kitchen, and disappearing down the cellar stairs. The cellar was full of water, and the door into the drain was wide open.

'The drain's flooded!' pronounced Mr Price, not without certain satisfaction. 'Her ladyship never let me repair it proper. It's six weeks now since she's been gone and nobody has heard a word from her wherever she took herself to. She's maybe gone abroad.'

Sir Ernest's reply was to hurry back to the car for a powerful torch. The footprints went down the steps, but they did not come back again. Hardly listening to the last part of Mr Price's information he felt sure that the footprints must belong to his wife, and without wasting another word he plunged into the stream and entered the drain at the same moment when the piercing yells of the bogwoppits, combined with Lady Clandorris's shouts and Samantha's screams, came echoing back out of the darkness.

Mr Price instinctively filled a couple of buckets that were floating about the cellar, dashed in some generous measures of disinfectant, and sent it swirling down the drain. The marsh water was just beginning to flow backwards as the rain had ceased. It carried the disinfectant down the current as it receded, pursuing the bogwoppits, who swam for their lives to safety.

The One-and-Only had actually suffered very little damage from the first flow that reached him, for the mixture was already much diluted by the flood water. But the smell and the possible consequences had so affected the bogwoppit's nerves that it fainted quite genuinely from sheer hysteria.

When they had all arrived back in the kitchen Mr Price went straight off to open the sluice gate below the marsh pools that would carry the extra flood water away.

Samantha with her aunt and her uncle waded out of the cellar into the hall, the bogwoppit hanging like a sodden leech on Samantha's arm.

'Who did you say this girl is?' Uncle Ernest said, puzzled, staring at Samantha.

'My niece. Our niece. My sister Gertie's girl, Samantha. She is the bravest child I have ever met and she cares for me very much indeed!' said Lady Clandorris.

'How do you do, Samantha!' said her Uncle Ernest. 'Very pleased to meet you!'

'How do you do!' replied Samantha. 'Please, if you will excuse me I will just go upstairs and give the bogwoppit a bath.'

20. Today and Tomorrow

'GIVE what a bath?' said Sir Ernest Clandorris when Samantha had gone upstairs.

'The bogwoppit,' said Lady Clandorris. 'It is an exceptionally intelligent and affectionate animal and Samantha is very attached to it. The bogwoppit cares for me too. It cares for me very much indeed.'

'A *bogwoppit*!' exclaimed Sir Ernest, looking completely amazed and incredulous. 'But bogwoppits have been extinct for the last two centuries or more, until . . .'

'They are certainly not extinct!' said Lady Clandorris tartly. 'There is a whole colony of them living in the drains of this house! And a whole colony of preservationists camped out in the Park taking pictures of them. And a whole colony of television and broadcasting people taking pictures of the other people taking pictures of the bogwoppits. Or so the bogwoppits tell me!' she added.

Sir Ernest looked at her closely. 'You don't mean to tell me you can understand their language?' he said.

'Of course I do!' said Lady Clandorris. 'You couldn't live with them for six or seven weeks without picking some of it up!'

'You astonish me!' said Sir Ernest.

'You may well be astonished,' his wife agreed. 'You didn't know I had been kidnapped, did you? I might have been left down the drain there for ever, for all you cared!'

'But I did care!' said Sir Ernest, reproachfully. 'I came all the way home from the heart of the

Amazonian jungle in South America to find you. I want you to come back with me to study the bogwoppits.'

'The *what*?' said Lady Clandorris.

'I found some in a marsh pool in the jungle!' said Sir Ernest. 'I even watched them hatching. But I want to find out a whole lot more about them before I report it to the British Museum. I've built a little hut there, far away from anywhere, just the sort of little place you would like. I know you never liked living in the Park. You know you could have come with me before, when I first went. *I asked* you to. You know I did!'

'I thought you were going with a party!' snapped Lady Clandorris.

'Well, I soon left them. Too much chatter!' said Sir Ernest. 'But what about it, old girl? We used to get along quite nicely once. I rather missed our yelling matches when there was nothing to shout at but the bogwoppits.'

'Probably you can't speak their language,' said Lady Clandorris smugly.

'Well if *you* can, Daisy, I can't do without you!' said Sir Ernest. 'You have got to come back to the Amazonian jungle with me.'

'But what about Samantha?' said Lady Clandorris. 'She wants me too.'

'Samantha can come with us!' said Sir Ernest expansively.

'No I can't!' said Samantha, coming downstairs with the bogwoppit wrapped in a towel and looking happier. She had been listening to the conversation. 'I have got to go to school, and I wouldn't want to drop behind all my friends in education. Besides, I like living at the Park. Why have you got to go all the way to South America when you can study all the bogwoppits you want to in the marsh pools? It doesn't make sense. Why don't you both just live here with me and the bogwoppit?'

'The bogwoppit can come to South America with us,' said Lady Clandorris.

'No it can't,' said Samantha firmly. 'It is a British bogwoppit and the South American ones might kill it. Besides, I'm not going to South America!'

'You are!' said Lady Clandorris.

'I'm not!' said Samantha.

At that moment there was a loud and very rusty ringing of the front door bell. Samantha deposited the bogwoppit on a chair and went to answer the door.

It was Mr Price to say that the sluice gate was open and should have emptied all the water out of the cellar by now. Also that the bogwoppits seemed to be as lively as ever in the marsh pools, and should he dowse them all with disinfectant.

'NO,' said Sir Ernest and Samantha together very loudly.

While Samantha and Lady Clandorris went on arguing about the One-and-Only and

going or not going to South America Mr Price
and Sir Ernest went to investigate the state of
the cellar below.

When they came back it appeared that Sir
Ernest had asked Mr Price to build a solid
cement partition at the cellar entrance to the
drain, with no bars and no gate and no lock
to it, so that the bogwoppits could not come
in and it could never be opened again.

'Then you can go and study them in the
Park!' said Samantha hopefully to her Uncle
Ernest.

'What? With all those perishing amateurs
and the Press breathing down my neck?'
scoffed Sir Ernest. 'Not me! Not likely! No
privacy in England, not even in my own Park.
I'm going back to South America to study
them in peace.'

'And so am I!' said Lady Clandorris. 'And
Samantha and the bogwoppit can come with us.'

'No!' said Samantha, and it began all over
again. Mr Price slipped tactfully away to

work out plans for the Great Wall inside the drain.

The argument went on and on, not very bitterly – in fact the longer it lasted the more Samantha felt that she was in the middle of a family row, and it was happening because nobody wanted to leave anybody behind. This was such a new sensation for Samantha that she hoped the argument would go on for ever. Even the bogwoppit seemed to be enjoying it.

Everyone paused for breath, but Lady Clandorris recovered first, and the solution that she offered was much the same as she had suggested to Samantha down in the great chamber of the drain.

'Samantha shall have the Park!' she announced. 'She loves it, and we don't. So she shall stay and look after it while we are in South America and she can be educated at the same time. We'll ask her Mr and Mrs Price to come and be caretakers. The grounds can be a safari park for bogwoppits. It will have to be

properly run and the public must be charged
for entrance. Mrs Price can give them tea.
Samantha can show them round the house.
They'll have to pay of course.'

Sir Ernest looked round the shabby walls
with some disapproval.

'What are they going to see?' he asked
discouragingly.

'It shall be redecorated and done up!' said
Lady Clandorris grandly. 'And there are all
those fascinating antiques in the upstairs
bedrooms. Samantha can choose the
wallpapers. And we'll come back at Christmas
and at Easter and Samantha can come out to
us in the summer holidays. Or else we'll come
back and shut up the safari park and just be
ourselves!'

'No we won't!' said Sir Ernest. 'We'll have
everybody in and Samantha can have a
birthday party whenever she likes, and we'll
show the public our slides of South America.
There are lots of things in the jungle besides

extinct bogwoppits. In my hut, for instance, I have a baby molypiddle.'

'A *what*?' exclaimed Samantha and Lady Clandorris together.

'A molypiddle. Furry, soft, batlike. But they only have one ear. Much cleaner than bogwoppits but very affectionate once they are tamed.'

'If you have a molypiddle you won't need the bogwoppit,' said Samantha.

'Yes I shall,' Lady Clandorris argued.

'You had better let the bogwoppit decide for itself,' said Sir Ernest Clandorris. He prodded the One-and-Only awake.

Samantha and Lady Clandorris stood with their arms opened wide, beseeching it. The bogwoppit shook the towel away, and stretched its wings, now fluffy and dry again. Then it stood on the tips of its toes, rose rapidly into the air with its familiar whirring flight, and dropped straight into Samantha's triumphant arms.

'Oh well!' said Lady Clandorris, stamping her foot and turning her back. But at that moment Sir Ernest took out of his pocket book a picture to show her of the lonely hut in the far off Amazonian jungles of South America. There was a molypiddle sitting on the roof.

Sir Ernest and Lady Clandorris (she had changed her clothes and was dressed quite smartly) with Samantha and the bogwoppit, went to discuss their plans with the Prices.

At first Mr and Mrs Price were unwilling to commit themselves, but by the next morning Jeff Price met Samantha in some excitement, saying he thought his parents were about to give in.

'Dad's got all worked up about having those drains to do as he likes with!' said Jeff. 'And Mum, well she quite likes the idea of putting the house to rights.'

'What about you and Deb and Timothy?' Samantha asked. 'Shall you mind leaving number fifty-four?'

'You bet we don't!' said Jeff enthusiastically. 'We haven't got room for a pianola!'

Mr Beaumont was called in and papers were signed. Builders and decorators were summoned, and Mr Price found himself directing quite a battalion of plumbers.

A postcard arrived from Aunt Lily and Duggie hoping that Samantha was getting on fine, because they were. If she ever wanted to join them she could. They wouldn't mind.

Samantha wrote back: 'My Aunt Daisy and my Uncle Ernest Clandorris say that I can live at the Park for the rest of my life.'

'It's no good expecting *me* to send you a postcard from South America!' Aunt Daisy said. 'And you needn't bother to send me one either. There are no post offices in the jungle, and as you know, I never look inside a mail box.'

At the thought that they would not be able to send each other postcards the most extraordinary thing happened. Lady Clandorris and Samantha both burst into tears and flew into each other's arms.

'We've made over the Park to you, Samantha!' hiccuped Lady Clandorris, extricating herself from Samantha and the bogwoppit, who wanted to be wept over too. 'Just in case something happens to your uncle or me while we are in South America. Mr Beaumont has it in writing. You are our heiress. It is all, every bit of it, yours!'

'*Mine?*' said Samantha. 'The house and the Park and the cellars and the woods? All of it?'

'All of it!' nodded Lady Clandorris.

'Even the bogwoppits?' said Samantha.

'And the bogwoppits!' agreed Lady Clandorris. 'Except the . . .'

'All the bogwoppits!' cried Samantha with her eyes shining. 'Especially the One-and-Only! He's the only one that really counts! Oh how *good* you are to me, Aunt Daisy!'

Sir Ernest and Lady Clandorris drove away on a day in early September, amid tears from Samantha and the One-and-Only.

The tears soon dried, for life turned out as Samantha had always dreamed and plotted that it would and ought to do.

The Park really belonged to her. She had birthday parties there, for herself, and for the Prices, and even for the bogwoppit. The house became beautiful under the decorators and clean and shining under Mrs Price. The drains were completely reorganized giving no more trouble.

The One-and-Only forgot how much it had liked dirt, and became quite fond of soap and water. It never showed the slightest interest in the bogwoppits in the marsh pools, but followed Samantha when she was at home, and Mrs Price when Samantha was at school.

The other bogwoppits remained the centre of scientific research for some time, and then Miss Mellor's Project was finished, while the

Preservation Society and the Press and the television company faded away.

By this time the marsh pools had been turned into a safari park so the bogwoppits still had plenty of people to show off to. Mrs Price made and served most delicious teas to the visitors in the stables, helped by Samantha and Deborah. Samantha showed parties of twenty round the house.

Every holiday Sir Ernest and Lady Clandorris came back to stay with Samantha at the Park, and her uncle insisted that the local Flower Show and Garden Fête should be held there. It was opened by Lady Clandorris, and everybody clapped her which to her surprise she enjoyed very much indeed. The One-and-Only presented her with a bouquet and everybody clapped *it*.

One summer Samantha went to stay in the Amazonian jungle with her aunt and uncle, leaving the bogwoppit behind for fear of reprisal. She found the South American bogwoppits fascinating (their eyes were green, not blue), though quite a bit different, and also the molypiddles, the clunkers, the dibs and debs, and all the other creatures that her Uncle Ernest was studying.

And she knew that, for all her aunt's odd manners and her tartness, she was Lady Clandorris's favourite niece (or why would she have left her the Park?) and her uncle's sweet Samantha, and they were her nearest and dearest and her own real and proper blood relations. But for true companionship and devotion and sympathy and affection she had (besides Mr and Mrs Price and Deborah, Jeff and Timothy), the everlasting loyalty and affection of the One-and-Only-Bogwoppit-in-the-World.

ABOUT THE AUTHOR
URSULA MORAY WILLIAMS

URSULA MORAY WILLIAMS

BOGWOPPIT

A PUFFIN BOOK

1911   *Born 19 April in Petersfield, Hampshire*

1927   *Attends school in Annecy, in France, for a year*

1928   *Enrols at the Royal College of Art in Winchester, but drops out to pursue her writing career*

1931   Jean Pierre, *Ursula's first book about a small boy and his pet goat, is published*

1932   *Ursula becomes a Brown Owl in the Brownies, inspiring her next two books*

1938   Adventures of the Little Wooden Horse *is published*

1942   Gobbolino the Witch's Cat *is published*

1943   The Good Little Christmas Tree *is published*

1945   *Moves to Beckford, near Evesham in South Worcestershire, where she serves as a magistrate for more than twenty years*

1970   *Ursula attends the first 'Puffin Winter Whoopee' in a castle and becomes a key member of the Puffin Club*

1978   Bogwoppit *is published and illustrated by renowned illustrator, Shirley Hughes*

1978   *A copy of* Gobbolino *is buried in the Puffin Time Capsule and will not be dug up until 2078! Ursula wrote a message in this book and no one knows what it says . . .*

1984   *Contributes to the children's TV show* Jackanory

2006   *Dies on 17 October in Tewkesbury, Worcestershire*

ABOUT THE ILLUSTRATOR

SHIRLEY HUGHES

Photograph by Eamonn McCabe

Shirley Hughes is one of the best-loved illustrators in the UK. She has written and illustrated many books for children and has won the Kate Greenaway Medal and the prestigious Eleanor Farjeon Award. In 1998 she was awarded the OBE for Services to Children's Literature. Shirley says: 'The project of illustrating Ursula Moray Williams's Bogwoppit *was irresistible . . . Every child is fascinated (as I was) by what might be living down there in the slime. This story gives full rein to hair-raising underground adventures . . . I was spoilt for choice as to which exciting incident to illustrate!'*

INTERESTING FACTS

Ursula Moray Williams was the author and illustrator of more than seventy books for children.

She continued to be published throughout the Second World War, making her one of the few children's authors who did so despite the paper shortages at that time.

Ursula was an identical twin!

WHERE DID THE STORY COME FROM?

Ursula loved writing about mischievous but good-hearted children based on those she saw during her work as a juvenile magistrate and a school governor. Many of her stories involved brave children or creatures who triumph over hardships and cruelty before finding a loving home. Park House is based on North Stoneham House, a large, dilapidated mansion where Ursula grew up.

GUESS
WHO?

A ... something hopped and shuffled into the room, something round and black and furry, with large, round, blue appealing eyes and a long furry tail ...

B And here she lay on her back in her bedroom, making a noise like a combine harvester ...

C ... first a large pair of safari boots, then the rising curves of a fairly big stomach, covered in a tweed suit, and finally a round face, pinkish red, even in the shadows, topped by a deerstalker's hat ...

D 'Furry, soft, batlike. But they only have one ear. Much cleaner than bogwoppits but very affectionate once they are tamed.'

WORDS GLORIOUS WORDS!

*Lots of **words** have several different meanings – here are a few you'll find in this Puffin book. Use a **dictionary** or look them up online to find other definitions.*

ancestral *something belonging to older generations of somebody's family*

wainscot *the bottom part of the walls in a room*

pianola *a piano that plays music by itself*

fragment *a piece of something*

deserted *a place that has been left with no one staying behind*

marsh *an area of land that is wet all the time*

monotonous *boring due to repetition*

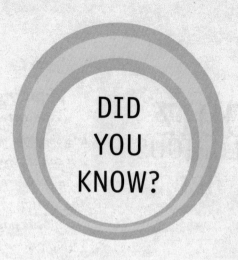

DID
YOU
KNOW?

Four of Ursula Moray Williams's stories were featured on the programme Jackanory, *where* celebrities read stories.

Bogwoppits don't really exist!

The Wildlife and Countryside Act of 1981 protects *rare animal and plant species in Great Britain, including* red squirrels *and* water voles.

QUIZ

Thinking caps on – let's see how much you can remember! Answers are at the bottom of the opposite page. (No peeking!)

1 **Why does Samantha go to live at Park House?**

a) *Her parents died*

b) *She ran away from home*

c) *Her parents are on holiday*

d) *Her Aunt Lily left her and went to America*

2 **Who are Samantha's best friends?**

a) *The Princes*

b) *The Prices*

c) *The Pringles*

d) *The Mellors*

3 What did Lady Clandorris use to get rid of the bogwoppits?

a) *A broom*

b) *Disinfectant*

c) *Bleach*

d) *Music*

4 What does the S.P.R.R.S. stand for?

a) *The Society for the Protection of Rare and Rural Species*

b) *The Super Physical Racing Response Station*

c) *The Station of Plenty of Rat and Rabbit Species*

d) *The Society for the Protection of Ringo the Rattle Snake*

5 Where did Uncle Ernest find more bogwoppits?

a) *Sri Lanka*

b) *South Africa*

c) *South America*

d) *New Zealand*

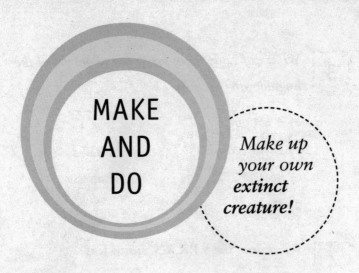

MAKE AND DO

*Make up your own **extinct creature!***

Draw a picture and create a fact file describing your creature's features, where it lives and what it likes to eat. Perhaps it has the ability to communicate with you in a special way too?

IN THIS YEAR

1978
Fact Pack

What else was happening in the world when this Puffin book was published?

URSULA MORAY WILLIAMS

BOGWOPPIT

NASA selects its **first** *women astronauts!*

The Incredible Hulk *is shown for the first time.*

May Day is a public holiday for the first time.

PUFFIN
WRITING
TIP

Write a description of your hometown –
as if you were talking to an alien.

If you have enjoyed reading *Bogwoppit* you may like to read *Gobbolino the Witch's Cat* in which Gobbolino searches for the home of his dreams . . .

1. Gobbolino in Disgrace

ONE FINE moonlight night little Gobbolino, the witch's kitten, and his sister Sootica tumbled out of the cavern where they had been born, to play at catch-a-mouse among the creeping shadows.

It was the first time they had left the cavern, and their round eyes were full of wonder and excitement at everything they saw.

Every leaf that blew, every dewdrop that glittered, every rustle in the forest around them set their furry black ears a-prick.

'Did you hear that, brother?'

'Did you see that, sister?'

'I saw it! *And that! and that! and that!*'

When they were tired of playing they sat side by side in the moonlight talking and quarrelling a little, as a witch's kittens will.

'What will you be when you grow up?' Gobbolino asked, as the moon began to sink behind the mountains and cocks crowed down the valley.

'Oh, I'll be a witch's cat like my ma,' said Sootica. 'I'll know all the Book of Magic off by heart and learn to ride a broomstick and turn mice into frogs and frogs into guinea-pigs. I'll fly down the clouds on the night-wind with the bats and the barn owls, saying "*Meee-ee-ee-oww!*" so when people hear me coming they'll say: "*Hush! There goes Sootica, the witch's cat!*"'

Gobbolino was very silent when he heard his sister's fiery words.

'And what will you be, brother?' asked Sootica agreeably.

'I'll be a kitchen cat,' said Gobbolino. 'I'll sit by the fire with my paws tucked under my chest and sing like the kettle on the hob. When the children come in from school they'll pull my ears and tickle me under the chin and coax me round the kitchen with a cotton reel. I'll mind the house and keep down the mice and watch the baby, and when all the children are in bed I'll creep on my missus's lap while she darns the stockings and master nods in his chair. I'll stay with them for ever and ever, and they'll call me Gobbolino the kitchen cat.'

'Don't you want to be bad?' Sootica asked him in great surprise.

'No,' said Gobbolino, 'I want to be good and have people love me. People don't love witches' cats. They are too disagreeable.'

He licked his paw and began to wash his face, while his little sister scowled at him and was just about to trot in and find their mother, when a ray of moonlight falling across both the kittens set her fur standing on end with rage and fear.

'Brother! Brother! one of your paws is white!'

In the deeps of the witch's cavern no one had noticed that little Gobbolino had been born with a white front paw. Everyone knows this is quite wrong for witches' kittens, which are black all over from head to foot, but now the moonbeam lit up a pure white sock with five pink pads beneath it, while the kitten's

coat, instead of being jet black like his sister's, had a faint sheen of tabby, and his lovely round eyes were blue! All witches' kittens are born with green eyes.

No wonder that little Sootica flew into the cavern with cries of distress to tell her mother all about it.

'Ma! Ma! Our Gobbolino has a white sock! He has blue eyes! His coat is tabby, not black, and he wants to be a kitchen cat!'

The kitten's cries brought her mother Grimalkin to the door of the cavern. Their mistress, the witch, was not far behind her, and in less time than it takes to tell they had knocked the unhappy Gobbolino head over heels, set him on his feet again, cuffed his ears, tweaked his tail, bounced him, bullied him, and so bewildered him that he could only stare stupidly at them, blinking his beautiful blue eyes as if he could not imagine what they were so angry about.

At last Grimalkin picked him up by the scruff of his neck and dropped him in the darkest, dampest corner of the cavern among the witch's tame toads.

Gobbolino was afraid of the toads and shivered and shook all night.

2. Gobbolino is Left Alone

IN THE morning Gobbolino heard the witch talking things over with his mother.

'I think we ought to apprentice the kittens very quickly,' she said. 'There is Sootica, who is eager to learn, and will make a clever little cat, while the sooner the nonsense is knocked out of her brother's head the better.'

So when the moon rose round and full the witch and her cat mounted their broomstick with the two young kittens in a bag slung behind them, and sailed away over the mountains to apprentice them to other witches, for that is the way to train a witch's cat.

They flew so fast, so fast, that little Gobbolino, peeping through a hole in the sack, saw the stars of the Milky Way flutter past him like a shower of diamonds – so fast that the bats they overtook seemed to lumber along like clumsy elephants.

It made him dizzy to look below him at the sleeping hills and rivers, the chasms and lakes, the watchful mountains and brooding cities. Little Sootica mewed for joy at their wild and giddy flight, but Gobbolino shivered at the bottom of the sack, while tears of terror dropped on his white front paw.

'Oh, please, stop! Oh, please, please, please!' he sobbed, but nobody paid any attention to him.

At last with a glorious swoop like the dive of a wild sea-bird, the witch and her broomstick came down on the Hurricane Mountains, where lived a hideous witch who agreed almost at once to take little Sootica into her cavern and train her as a witch's cat.

The kitten was so overjoyed she could hardly stop to say goodbye to her little brother, she was so eager to begin learning how to turn people into toads and frogs and other disagreeable objects.

Gobbolino cried a little at parting with his playmate, but the witch quite refused to take him with his sister.

'A witch's cat with a white paw! Ho! ho! ho!' she croaked. 'You'll never get rid of that one!'

So Gobbolino rode away on the broomstick once more, behind his mother Grimalkin and her mistress, and although they visited fifty or more caverns before the dawn broke over the Hurricane Mountains, not a witch would look twice at the kitten with the white paw and beautiful blue eyes.

So they flew home again and flung Gobbolino into the cavern among the toads, and there he stayed day after day, till one fine morning he woke up and found himself all alone.

The witch had gone and Grimalkin too, the cauldron, the book of spells, the toads, the foxes, the magic herbs, the brews, the broomstick, everything that had once made magic.

They had all flown away and deserted him for ever.

Gobbolino the Witch's Cat
is available in A Puffin Book.

A Puffin Book can take you to amazing places.

WHERE WILL YOU GO?

#PackAPuffin

A PUFFIN BOOK

stories that last a lifetime

Ever wanted a friend who could take you to magical realms, talk to animals or help you survive a shipwreck? Well, you'll find them all in the **A PUFFIN BOOK** collection.

A PUFFIN BOOK will stay with you **forever**. Maybe you'll read it again and again, or perhaps years from now you'll suddenly **remember** the moment it made you **laugh** or **cry** or simply see things **differently**. Adventurers **big** and **small**, rebels out to **change** their world, even a mouse with a **dream** and a spider who can spell – these are the characters who make **stories** that last a **lifetime**.

Whether you love animal tales, war stories or want to know what it was like growing up in a different time and place, the **A PUFFIN BOOK** collection has a story for you – you just need to decide where you want to go next . . .